Blood Kin

Ceridwen Dovey

Atlantic Books

LONDON

Essex County Council Libraries

First published as a trade paperback in Great Britain in 2007
by Atlantic Books, an imprint of Grove Atlantic Ltd.

This paperback edition pubished in Great Britain in 2008 by Atlantic Books.

9 8 7 6 5 4 3 2 1

A CIP catalogue record for this book is available from the British Library.

ISBN: 978 1 84354 658 0

Designed and typeset by Richard Marston
Printed in Great Britain

Atlantic Books
An imprint of Grove Atlantic Ltd
Ormond House
26–27 Boswell Street
London WC1N 3JZ

For Ken, Teresa and Lindiwe

PART I

1 *His portraitist*

He came every two months for a sitting. Always early in the day, usually on a Friday, when he still had something vital in his face from the week's effort, but a mellowness in his eyes from the knowledge it was almost over. In the late spring, the fallen jacaranda blossoms lay luminous on the pavement outside at that time of day, and his assistant would scoop them up by the handful and strew them over the couch where he sat, or lay, or lounged for each portrait. Regal purple petals. Made him feel like a king.

I always mixed my palette before he arrived. I knew the shade of his skin, the hue of his hair, the pinkness of the half-moons in his nails. After he'd arrived, and was seated, I'd adjust the colours slightly, according to his mood: if it had been a bad week, his skin tone needed more yellow; if he was feeling benevolent, I added a daub of blue to the white for his eyes. He said having his picture painted was his only therapy.

I would start with a charcoal sketch of his face. I was ruthless about detail, and documented each new wrinkle or discolouration or sausage spot, but this is what he wanted – in his very first sitting, I flattered him on the canvas, and he threatened never to return, so the next time I painted him as he was, and it pleased him. You would be surprised what can happen to a face in two months. One day I'll bind together all the surviving charcoal sketches and make a flipbook that jolts single frames into action when thumbed quickly. The flipbook's action will be the ageing of the President.

The oil portraits used to take me exactly six hours. He would decide on his pose, and when he had settled into it his assistant blotted his face oil with foundation and, on days when the President looked particularly tired, added some authority to his eyes with eyeliner. He had an uncanny ability to sit still for hours. At the end of each session, before the paint had even dried, his assistant collected the portrait to hang next to the flag in Parliament, so that the portrait in Parliament was always the most current, and the outdated ones were distributed to dignitaries to hang in their homes.

2 *His chef*

The President's favourite meal was Sunday brunch, when I would do a fresh seafood platter for him and serve it in the private dining room in his city apartment; not even his family joined him for this meal. We established a comfortable routine over the years. The guard would let me into the apartment at 9 a.m. I brought all the ingredients, uncooked, with me, and prepared the meal in his own kitchen, as quietly as I could, so as not to wake him. I had equipped the kitchen to meet my needs and did tasks there that I had long abandoned doing in the main Presidential Residence kitchens, things like disembowelling crayfish using their own feelers, destoppering sea snails, beheading prawns. These are normally jobs for lowly kitchen boys, but in his quiet kitchen on a Sunday I grew fond of doing my own dirty work – I communed with an earlier self that way, remembered my own humble beginnings; it reminded me of my respect for processes, the satisfaction of peeling and chopping and mincing and grating, all the myriad ways one can put a culinary world in order. I can't deny the pride I felt knowing that each item I prepared in that kitchen would nourish the President.

As soon as I arrived, I would place the live abalone on the floor of the pantry. They were always tense from being transported and had to calm down before I could kill them, otherwise the flesh would be tough. I would leave them there until everything else was almost ready, then creep up on them and hit them on their soft underbellies with the end of a rolling pin. If they sensed me coming they contracted like a heart muscle and were wasted.

3 *His barber*

The President was meticulous about his facial hair, same with his ear and nostril hair. He insisted that I use tweezers to dig deep into his orifices to root out the hair at its source, which inevitably inflicted pain, and he swore and threw things against the wall to cope, and afterwards panted like a dog in heat (I secretly suspected he liked it). He had a daily late-afternoon appointment with me in preparation for evening functions. His hair grew fast and blue and by the end of each day his stubble showed its colour, but the ear and nostril ritual I performed only weekly. Like all men, the President's favourite part of the session was the lathering – the brush I used was soft but firm, and the shaving soap lathered easily with moisture, needing little encouragement. I made small circles on his lower face until the soap foamed. I know it felt good.

For me, the satisfaction was in de-lathering. I would sharpen my knife in front of the President, and he would wince from the sound, but he never opened his eyes to look, which could be interpreted as a sign of either cowardice or bravery. Then I would take his head firmly between my hands and tilt it backwards. This was the moment I waited for each day: with a brisk twist of my hands, I could have snapped his neck, slit his throat with a knife-flick, but I did neither. I would start at the bottom of his neck with the blade and glide it slowly upwards, watching the stubble mingle with the foam.

Every evening the floor of my shop would be covered with hair. Hair is an extension of self – I believe it has power. When I looked at the hair of so many people lying tangled on the floor, it was like seeing earlier selves and discarded personality tics made manifest, so I never threw it away; my assistant swept it into a heap then bottled it to keep on shelves in the backroom.

4 *His portraitist*

I was forbidden by the President to paint any other person's portrait. This was the condition on which I was initially commissioned – he said my eye was always to be fresh for his face – and I agreed because the fee I received meant I needed to do no other paying work and could paint as I used to, when I was a student: only for myself and anybody who chose to be my audience.

My wife was the first to choose to be my audience. I had painted furiously for several months at university and hired out an industrial basement to exhibit my work. I was proud and believed good art speaks for itself, so I didn't advertise or print flyers or put an announcement in the student newspaper about the exhibition. But I hadn't seen friends during my painterly hibernation and my professors weren't sure that I still existed. Nobody came. I sat in the basement and drank the beer I'd bought alone. She appeared at the door (looking for a toilet, she told me years later) towards midnight – her shoulders narrower than her hips, her hair undyed, her collarbones drawing my eyes like magnets. I opened her a beer and let her browse my work while she sipped. She took a long time over my drawings, paying them attention they weren't used to in a room of oil paintings, slinking in and out of the pools of light thrown on each one, cocooned in her sequined slip. Eventually she went to the toilet at the back of the basement.

'It's not flushing,' she said. 'The handle is broken.'

At least, I thought, something of her will be left when she leaves. Later, after I'd fallen in love, everything about her – clipped nails she'd left in a jagged pile on the floor, her morning breath, her week-old underwear in the laundry basket – became a clue to her chemistry, and I began to believe that I could possess it, could possess her, if I were vigilant enough to collect all the clues. When she'd left the basement I stood above the toilet bowl and inhaled like a dog. I wet my finger and lifted a sequin from the floor.

My wife was also in the business of aesthetics – she was a food beautician, her speciality: hamburgers. She told me that they only ever film the front half of a burger; the back half looks like a construction site. She painted soft wax onto buns, placed individual sesame seeds strategically, and once sifted through two hundred lettuces to find the perfect frilled salad leaf to spray with silicon. The worst part about it, she always said, was watching an actor bite into the burger, having to smile full-mouthed with the wax starting to congeal on the roof of his mouth. She kept a special bucket for them to spit out what they'd chewed as soon as the camera stopped rolling.

One evening, dressing for dinner, she held up a photograph on a cardboard box from a pair of sheer stockings she'd just opened; a picture of a pair of legs in tights, the limbs long and beautiful.

'Do you think she has nice legs?' she asked me, and before I could respond said, 'You know that she is a he. All stocking models are men.'

She always warned me that things are not what they seem.

Now she is eight months pregnant and it kills me that I can't see her. Her hair had mushroomed thickly, her tummy was so taut that her belly button left an indent on anything she wore, and her nipples had spread like a pink stain across her breasts, claiming space. When they took her she only had time to put on her dressing gown. Her hair was still wet.

I should have known, at the last sitting, that something was wrong. The President had changed colour – every fibre of him was a tone I hadn't mixed on my palette before – and he scratched around on the settee like a fussy poodle making its nest for the night and wouldn't sit still. He brought his body-guards up to the studio when normally they waited in the foyer of my apartment building, and his assistant even forgot to collect the petals.

My wife was in the bath, the first ritual of her day, lying dead still, with just her belly protruding, and watching the baby's movements ripple the water. She could lie there for hours, transfixed.

The bodyguards were shot with silenced guns. They simply crumpled where they stood, like puppets a child has lost interest in. The President's assistant, without a word, opened my wardrobe, stepped into it and closed the mirrored door behind him quietly. It was only then that I saw them: two masked gunmen, slick as spiders, with their weapons trained on the President. I dropped my palette and raised my hands in supplication. I could hear my wife murmuring in the bathroom.

They motioned for me to move to the President's side. I sat next to him on the couch, our shoulders touching, with one gunman behind us, while the other moved towards the bathroom door.

'Please.' I only realized later that I whispered this. 'Please. Not her.'

He opened the door and for a few seconds stood watching her. I could see into the room from the couch. She didn't turn her head; she thought it was me. The gunman lifted her roughly from the bath in one movement and she stood naked, barefoot on the bathroom floor, screaming my name.

'Put on your dressing gown,' I whispered. 'Behind the door. Put it on.'

The silk clung to her and darkened around her breasts and stomach as she clutched the gown strings around her waist. The gunman forced her to walk in front of him, and as she approached me and the President sitting on the settee she dropped to her knees. He pulled her up again just as she was reaching out her arms to me. I strained for hers, but she only managed to grasp the President's hand. She screamed my name but clutched his hand, then she was gone, forced down the stairs and out of the foyer. The assistant wasn't discovered. I wonder if he is still hiding in my closet.

Now we are being held prisoner in one of the guestrooms of the President's Summer Residence – me, his chef and his barber – in a room too high above the ground to contemplate escape. We each have a bed with virgin linen so white I feel guilty sleeping in it, and there is an en-suite bathroom with silver fittings. A man brings bread, water, cheese and tomatoes to our door in the mornings and soup in the evenings. I haven't seen my wife since the day they took us, almost a week ago.

I was the first prisoner to be left in the room. They blindfolded me and the President in my apartment, forced us into a vehicle, and drove into the mountains – I know those spiralling roads too well to be fooled; the air thins and you start to drive faster from light-headedness, to overtake and stay for longer than you need to on the wrong side of the road. Those roads bring out the death wish in people. The President and I leaned into each other as the driver took the corners; his body is more pliable than I imagined.

We were separated at the Summer Residence – our blind-folds were removed and he was led away into the building, which I recognized immediately from postcards and magazine spreads; it was declared a national monument last year. I was led up many flights of stairs to the bedroom and left alone. The chef was brought in the afternoon, straight from the President's kitchens, where they were in the middle of making zabaglione for lunchtime dessert. His sous-chef was shot because he tried to sneak out of the delivery entrance, and the kitchen boys had stood gaping as the masked gunman bound the chef's wrists and blindfolded him. He still had dried egg on his hands when he arrived, and immediately ran himself a bath and sat in the bathroom with the door closed for a long time. The barber only arrived at dusk. He's taken the whole thing quite badly, and eventually talked himself to sleep.

From where I stand on the small balcony, I can see the valley below dimly in the moonlight, the only fertile ground in the country. It must be a new agricultural trend, to farm in circles – the fields are separated into massive green polka dots with a slice of yellow cut out of them, which makes them look like they are devouring each other. My wife and I came wine-tasting in the valley for her birthday, years ago. There were only two vineyards and the wine was close to awful, but once we were in the valley basin we felt newly created. It was summer and the hot air had collected at the bottom, and as we descended the mountain road to the valley base we peeled off layers of clothing; another layer for each drop in altitude, until we were almost naked and sweating and even the bad wine was soothing. The vineyard owner took us on a tour of the cellars and told us the monks had used underground caves to store their wine for hundreds of years, but gradually the caves were forgotten until a farmer out with a pack of hunting dogs stumbled upon one of the openings. He grandly revealed cobwebbed caskets of the original monks' wine, rendered undrinkable by years of imprisonment within glass; my wife persuaded him to let us smell it and it seemed to burn the hairs within my nostrils.

The chef is snoring like a stalling motor boat. Something else is bothering me, though, some noise of distress beneath the night sounds from the room, men's voices playing hide-and-seek. I trace them to the air vent above my bed, and stand on the mattress with my ear against the cold metal mesh.

'Did you... hundreds of... list them... their names?'

I pull on the mesh cover. It comes out of the wall, leaving the vent gaping in the darkness. The voices seem to be travelling upwards from the room beneath me.

'List each order... spare... burden... is my condition.'

Another man's voice disguised with pain rises to me and dissolves into grunts to ward off new blows to his stomach – or so I imagine, from his breathing. A door slams and a man heaves, his solar plexus in spasm.

I have avoided thinking about why I am here. I have never paid attention to politics; if I am exempt from one thing as an artist, surely it is knowing what my government is doing. Much more interesting to me than the puny stirrings of student revolutionaries was how to transform a thought into an image, how to paint the sky without using blue, how to get perspective wrong on purpose. My wife and I made it a rule never to listen to the news. 'It's all relative anyway,' she would say, imagining that politicians do to their actions what fast-food advertisers do to their burgers. It seemed purer to know nothing than to glean bits of information thrown to us like chum to sharks. We didn't even own a television set.

Perhaps that is not quite true. I was interested in politics long ago, growing up in a small family in the heart of the city's Presidential District. My parents paid attention to the news the way most people notice the weather, absent-mindedly, and I used to try to shake them out of their apathy. But after I'd met my wife my world seemed to shrink wonderfully, so that I needed nothing more than to see her immersed in a bathtub, her body refracted by the water, or to watch her lift a scream-ing kettle from the stove in one graceful arc, to be deliriously happy. She is the kind of woman you can never get tired of, for she is secretive and has a vivid internal life that is opaque to me. To observe her while she was concentrating on something else – a book, packing a suitcase, tying her shoelaces – was to ache with wonder.

She had her own reasons for choosing ignorance. Her father is a prominent farmer who owns the biggest prawn farm in the country and breeds sleek horses as abundantly as rabbits. He was wooed into politics just before we got married and became famous for using fire hoses instead of bullets to remove pro-testing students from a government building. People put his compassion down to his love of animals. His position meant the paparazzi attended our wedding as invited guests, and it was at his insistence that I got the job as presidential portraitist. The President had never been painted before, only photographed. My wife's father, quietly horrified at her choice of husband, organized for me to spend a weekend with the President at his coastal villa, painting his wife and his children, who were old enough to sit still for a watercolour. His wife had the same ability as he did to withstand an artist's scrutiny for hours, but she smelt like a fallen woman. The President sat in on part of her session and she became pert under his gaze, making me feel like a voyeur. Then she insisted I paint her husband too.

The voice from the air vent moans a name: my wife's name. It must be the President – his wife and mine share the same name although they are generations apart. I didn't recognize his voice at first, but trauma will do that to a man.

5 *His chef*

Morning has broken. I throw aside the curtains and look out at the valley below, my wrists still faintly ringed from rope-burn, and slice the tomatoes, cheese and bread that have been left just inside the doorway, using the sill as a table. The tomatoes are the kind that smell of sugar, valley tomatoes; in the city they arrive bruised and insolent. I wonder if the supermarkets have anything left on the shelves – on my blindfolded drive to the mountains I could hear the sounds of rioting in the streets around me, and somebody punched a fist through the rear window of the car; the driver swerved onto the pavement to escape, and hit somebody, or something, but didn't stop. Once we were out of the city, I could smell that the guards in the car were eating large chunks of matured cheese that should have been consumed in small and savoured doses.

I tear the loaf into three and close my eyes to conjure up the smell of coffee. I open them to find the portraitist looking directly at me, his face harrowed. I saw him last night standing on his bed in the dark, fiddling with the air vent; I suspect he's planning some kind of elaborate escape that will get him killed.

'Do you know,' he says quietly, 'why you're here?'

The barber and I look at him sharply. These are the first words he's uttered this morning.

'Regime change,' I respond. 'We just got caught in the middle of it, that's all.'

Maybe I shouldn't have said that so flippantly – he looks like he's taken it personally. The barber fidgets as if he has an unbearable itch, then stands, takes his share of the bread, and eats it quickly.

'They're only leaving us alone because they don't know what to do with us,' I continue. 'They can't figure out where we fit in.'

The barber closes the bathroom door and I hear him lower the toilet seat. My own bowels start to move in response. The portraitist has moved to the window and surprises me when he speaks again.

'Why would they take my wife, then? How does she fit in?'

'Pollution through association.'

He turns to look at me, hurt. 'But not my child. Not my unborn child.'

That would be too far even for me to go, so I leave him to stare out at the fields below. There is nothing to do but get back into bed and wait for the barber to leave the bathroom.

A key scrapes at the door and it opens to reveal a man standing in the corridor, dressed as if he's about to be taken sailing, in leather slippers that have become soft and oily at the places that rub against his heels, casual slacks, a dress shirt with the top four buttons undone. He is beautiful and I feel suddenly shy, but relieved to see the portraitist is also gaping. The barber chooses this moment to emerge from the bathroom, the toilet flushing noisily behind him. The man smiles, walks into the room and sits with his legs crossed on the couch facing the windows.

'Gentlemen,' he says.

He looks at us as if waiting for approval. I only manage to clear my throat and throw the bed covers to one side.

'Your wife is safe,' he says to the portraitist. 'You needn't worry about her, but you cannot see her until the child is born.'

The portraitist's face collapses with relief and fury and he swallows his tears.

'I apologize for the unintended similarity of your situation to the children's rhyme. What is it, butcher, baker, candlestick maker? Let me make it up to you by saying you can call me Commander. Equally ridiculous.'

He laughs with his eyes only.

I chanted that rhyme to my daughter when she was small, and it scared her witless. She couldn't bear the thought of those men bound together, stranded. She came home from school a few weeks later and told me they'd read about how a long time ago men were punished for doing bad things: a man would be tied in a sack with a monkey and a poisonous snake, then dropped overboard, and the three creatures would kill each other before they drowned. She said it reminded her of that rhyme I used to sing, the one about the three men stuck in a tub at sea.

'You won't be harmed. Each of you has spent many years perfecting a skill; we want you to make yourselves useful.' The Commander pauses, then looks directly at me. 'I want you to prepare dinner for me, starting tonight. You can make a list of ingredients you need.'

I am, despite myself, flattered, and my mind begins to whirr thinking of what I'll need. The barber looks at me in surprise, then with something like wry recognition; the portraitist is still struggling with his tears. The Commander stands and leaves the room, walking like a man who has had many women.

This week I will make for him what I learned to create first: pastry. My grandmother taught me. She would only come to stay with us in the hot months of the year and I loved her so much I would sneak into her room and sniff the dresses she left in the cupboard between stays – even now a wet facecloth reminds me of the smell of her stockings drying on the clothing rack. When I was about to get into trouble with my mother, I would run screaming to my grandmother, who would give me sweets instead of hidings. Pastry-making had to happen so early in the morning the summer sun hadn't yet risen. The night before we would fill glass bottles with water and stack them in the icebox and the dough would be left to rise under a dishcloth in the pantry. She would wake me just before dawn. She'd knead the dough and then begin to flatten it using a frozen glass bottle as a rolling pin, keeping the dough cool so the butter didn't melt too easily as it was rolled onto each layer. My task was to add new ice blocks to a bowl of water she dipped her hands into when they became warm and began to make the dough sticky.

In the town where I grew up there was a chocolate factory, and when different winds blew I could smell different chocolates being made. The north-easterly carried the smell of peppermint. In my second year of school my class went on an excursion to the factory and we were allowed to descend on the hexagonal cardboard bins at the end of each conveyor belt carrying finished chocolates to their wrappers. These bins were brimful with rejects – warped chocolate bars that had grown tumours or blistered or become stunted – but we swore this only made them taste more delicious, and the primal allure of all things deformed induced us to dig into the bin up to our armpits. Before we left, one of the boys somehow stuck his hand in a chocolate blender – a large machine that looked like it could mix concrete – and lost his pinkie. The floor manager could barely disguise his contempt for the child for ruining the batch. I was fascinated with the image of his blood mixing with the chocolate, and with the knowledge that our small class was the only keeper of the horrible secret. For months afterwards I was convinced that brand of chocolate bar had taken on a rusty tinge.

Tonight I will make the Commander paella. Paella only needs scraps of creatures, and I assume that is all that's going since the coup. I am interested in poor people's food: pizza, paella, minestrone, potato salad – these were all desperate creations, the end product of a search to make dregs of food palatable. One week when my father was unemployed we ate potato salad for every meal. Now it's acceptable to serve it at official functions, spruced up with capers or cured ham. I once called in an order for a thousand servings of the stuff for the President's summer banquet – a local potato farmer had his workers make it on the farm and the farmer drove it into the city in two trucks.

6 *His barber*

I called my home the glass box. It meant I could never throw stones, just like the proverb warned. I designed containers for everything so that things could be neatly tucked away and not clutter the surfaces. In my bathroom drawer, I had customized compartments for my toothbrush, floss, facewash, deodorant, razor. In my bedroom cupboard I kept my caps and glasses colour-coded and had small hollows for each belt to fit into, once rolled. I've never liked lying down on my bed in my street clothes, even with my shoes off (I believe it pollutes my sleep), I always leave a window open at night, no matter how cold it is, and I can't bear leaving my home for a long trip if there is any dirty linen or clothing in it. If I know I have to go away somewhere for a while, I lay out the clothes I'm going to wear, take off the clothes I'm wearing, put them in the washing machine with my sheets and walk around naked until it's almost time to leave. That's why I was naked when they took me: ready for my trip, about to put on my clean travelling clothes, and next thing there was a man in my laundry pointing a gun at me.

The chef has given me the task of washing a bucketful of mussels; I have to check that each one is firmly shut – if it has opened in the bucket it is dangerous to eat and I'm supposed to throw it out. The portraitist is de-boning fish. We are the chef's kitchen boys for the night and the chef is transformed; he has completely lost himself in the logistics of preparing a meal and is cackling like a smug housewife over a pot of rice. The kitchen is as large as one would expect in a summer residence used primarily to entertain. We were escorted here by two men – armed, but dressed like they had just got back from the office. The chef couldn't resist telling them the menu for the evening, but they didn't respond. Somebody had managed to find fresh seafood and every other item on the chef's ingredient wish-list, and it was waiting for us in the kitchen in paper bags. He was like a small child on his birthday, going through the bags gleefully; then he did a quick spot-check of the kitchen equipment and found it all to his satisfaction. The two armed men have stayed in the kitchen, perched on kitchen stools with their backs against the wall, watching that we don't poison the food.

'I've worked here before,' the chef says, stirring the rice. 'Many years ago. I came with my wife at the time, and we spent a month living in one of the suites. I experimented on the President – pushed his tastes, fed him wild meats, foreign fruit. He liked that I pushed him. Most people around him wouldn't dare.'

He takes the knife from the portraitist and fillets a fish effortlessly.

I find three mussels, still in a hoary clump, that have opened in the bucket, and throw them aside. The odour of raw fish reminds me of my brother, of what he would come home stinking of at lunchtime. He was older than me by ten years, and, sitting at the round table in the kitchen with my mother,

23

eating crustless sandwiches and telling her about my morning at school, I would smell him coming before I heard the door slam. He would wash off stray fish scales from his hands at the tap outside and rinse and remove his boots, and come into the kitchen in wet socks. My mother would hover about him like an anxious bee about the queen, ladle out a hot lunch she had cooked, ask about his catch. He left so early in the mornings the gulls weren't even awake and went out on a borrowed trawler for the nine hours it took to catch enough fish to make a living. If we were lucky he would bring a bunch of small fish for our supper, but my mother never asked him outright, we just waited to see if he would volunteer them from his canvas bag once he had eaten lunch. At school in the afternoon I could still smell him on my pencil case and sometimes on my hands if he had agreed to play aeroplanes.

It broke my mother when he disappeared. I was older then, and not paying anybody but myself much attention. I hadn't even really registered his absence. It was only when she sat down one lunchtime and put her head on the table and wouldn't eat anything that I realized he hadn't eaten meals with us in over two weeks. For a long time we thought he had eloped with his fiancée – she disappeared with him – but I couldn't understand why none of his crew had come to tell us. They avoided us at the market and at the dock. My mother stopped getting dressed in the mornings.

It was on my birthday that the letter arrived. It was from him, but had been posted almost a year before, and he had written only one sentence: 'Taken captive political prisoner we'll be fine.' That letter lit a fire beneath my mother and she went visiting – old friends, close family, vague family, ex-girlfriends

24

– until she had pieced together a patchwork of possibilities. It turned out he and his fiancée had been active in some kind of underground resistance movement. His fishing crew had never approved, said he was asking for trouble. The second letter arrived two months later. It wasn't from my brother. The writer, anonymous, told us that my brother's body had been buried in the mountains. The writer said he – or she – was sorry.

The chef has put on full serving gear that he found in the pantry, even the hat, which makes him look like he has dough rising slowly on his head. My task during the meal is to pour the water and wine for the Commander, but the portraitist refuses to serve him and says he'll wait in the kitchen. The chef alone will serve the food. He uses his shoulder to bump the swinging doors into the dining room and walks ceremoniously towards the Commander, who is seated at a small, square table in the centre of the room. The long dining table has been moved aside and a single place is set. The Commander smiles at the chef and smirks at me dutifully carrying a bottle of wine in a bucket of ice. The cork is so stubborn I am tempted to put the bottle between my legs and pull on it, but instead I put it under my arm and tug. The chef places a napkin on the Commander's lap with flair. My job is done; I leave the room.

The portraitist is standing at the kitchen window, staring down into the courtyard. He is in agony: I have never seen an emotion made so manifest.

'My wife,' he says. 'She's here. She's being kept here. I saw her in the courtyard.'

I place my hand on his shoulder gently. 'Is this not a good thing? You know she is being looked after. You know where she is.'

He turns to me and, before I can move away, has put his head against my chest. His grief spreads across my shirt, heating it.

'I called to her from up here. I opened the window and called down to her. She was alone, sitting on that bench. She looked up at me like a stranger, then she stood and walked away.'

I imagine I know why she did this, something about the pollution thing the chef said to him this morning. I pat his head awkwardly, but I am no good at consoling. When he shifts his head I move away towards the swinging doors to listen to what the Commander is saying to the chef. His fork makes scratchy music against his plate.

'You have excelled yourself.'

The chef murmurs deferentially. The scraping stops, the plate has been licked clean.

'And do you have a wife?' The Commander asks this the way one would speak to a small child, with bored patience and no expectation of a reply.

If the chef is surprised, his voice doesn't betray him. 'Ex-wife. Haven't seen her for months.' He stops, uncertain how much the Commander is willing to listen to.

'Ah. Why did you divorce?'

The chef pauses. 'She went crazy,' he says, his tone ironic. 'Became obsessed with energy flow. Made me knock down three walls in our house because she said they were blocking peace lines.'

The Commander laughs loudly.

7   *His portraitist*

We slept together for the first time in the afternoon. That was always her favourite time of day for sex – we would eat lunch on my balcony, drink a beer, and then lie on the bed, the heat and sleepiness in itself arousing. She didn't want me to use any protection because she took her own temperature every morning and knew exactly when she was ovulating. She kept a small thermometer and a notebook beside her bed, and in the morning she'd sit up, her hair like a mane, and before she'd even opened her eyes she'd open her mouth and sit with the mercury beneath her tongue, waiting. Then she'd squint to look at the reading, write it down, and walk naked to the toilet. I loved how her thighs shuddered as she walked. She would stand at the basin, brushing her teeth, and mumble through the foam, asking me what I wanted for breakfast, or whether I was planning to work in the studio. I couldn't answer, transfixed by the sight of her, her stomach separating into three bulges as she bent to rinse out her mouth. I wanted to communicate the extent of my love for her in those moments, but was afraid she would baulk at my neediness, or interpret it as something too consuming and try to resist.

One afternoon we used protection because her body

temperature was a degree higher than normal, but it broke inside her; I felt the pressure give. We went to a clinic together, but I had to wait in the outside waiting room while she was let into the inner sanctum after being frisked. Security was tight. She came out after an hour, clutching a small booklet with two pills in it: one she had to take immediately, one in the middle of the night. When midnight struck, I didn't even hear the alarm, and only woke when she shook my arm – she was on her hands and knees on the bedroom floor, searching in a panic for the pill she'd dropped in the dark. In our sleepy confusion we didn't think to switch on the light. I leaned over the side of the bed while she scoured the floor with her hands, reaching into the gap beneath the skirting. Then she felt something and lifted it on her palm. The pill was tiny. She swallowed it and crawled back into bed and we held each other as if we'd just escaped certain death.

I'm waiting for the voices. The chef and the barber fell asleep long ago; they sleep like babies, guiltless. I have already removed the casing from the air vent above the bed. I'm trying not to think of how she looked at me from the courtyard.

'Freedom… your life.'

Here they are. That is the Commander, I can recognize his voice now.

'Stay… power… better for everybody. Come to me then… talk about sacrifice.'

It sounds as if papers are being thrown onto the floor.

'Have… witness.'

I hear the door slam, and then footsteps on the stairs. I hold my breath. Someone unlocks the door and a man pulls me soundlessly from the bed. I follow him docilely, barefoot down the stairs, wondering if I should have screamed to wake the others.

The Commander stands at an open door in a silk dressing gown made for a man and I remember what my wife looked like as she was taken out of the apartment. The President is shirtless, sitting on a couch in the middle of the room. It is strewn not with petals, but with photographs, hundreds of them upholstering the sides and patterning the floor at his feet. His face is broken in places, his nose swollen. He keeps his legs tightly together, his hands in his lap, and it is only as I get closer that I see that his wrists are still bound. It is dreadful to look at him, but my eyes can't help sliding back to the sight. The man shuts the door behind me and locks it.

'Sit next to him,' the Commander says to me. 'Push some of those aside and sit on the couch.'

I look at the purple bloom on the President's chest and imagine being winded by a fist, then I lift a handful of photographs and manage not to look at them as I put them on the floor.

The Commander sits in an armchair facing us. He props his feet on the coffee table between us and yawns. 'This man sitting next to you, I want you to hand him one of the photos.'

I look directly at the Commander, feel with my left hand for a photograph without looking down, and put it on the couch next to the President. The Commander's fatigue leaves him as I watch, the way a demon leaves a man possessed.

'Look at the photograph.' He pulls on his chin, fiercely coiled for attack.

Can I will myself not to see when my eyes are open? No. The man's face in the photograph is a failed pudding, flabby and flecked with blood, his head making an obscene angle with his spine. After I've seen it, I turn to pass it to the President, forgetting his hands are bound.

'Hold it for him, would you? Make his job a little easier.' The Commander has leaned forward in his armchair.

The photo quivers in my hand – it must have a will of its own – and the President clears his throat, but says nothing. The Commander leans back in his chair, pensive. I let go of the photo and it drops with deadweight to the floor. The President lifts his chin as a warning, but it comes too late, and something connects with my torso at the level of my kidneys until they scream their trauma throughout my body. I cough and spit onto the photos pooled at my feet. I refuse to look behind me, but I can hear the henchman retreat to the shadows. All the blood in my body has left my brain, my tongue; it has been drawn to my kidneys to help them haemorrhage. I lick my lips. The pain has made me fearless. Until it passes, I care nothing about what they do or say to me.

Even pain makes me think of her. The night we spent in a run-down guesthouse on holiday, where we stood in the bath in sandals, afraid of what we might catch barefoot, and washed each other with the handheld hose. There was no hot water. I tried to warm her under the sheets by lying stomach-down on her back, pressing her into the mattress. I had a cyst on the inside of my wrist, a small lump between the veins. She'd heard that cysts can be cured if you put extreme pressure on them, so, in the dark, I held out my wrist, closed my eyes, locked my jaw, and she pressed her finger as hard as she could against the cyst. It throbbed unbearably the rest of the night, but in the morning the lump was gone.

8 *His chef*

It is Sunday. The crayfish will be crouched in their buckets waiting for me, the abalone will be tight as marble, piled on top of each other, contracted against contact, and it will take a while to soothe them. I touch the portraitist's forearm to wake him and he starts and looks at me, hurt – he still hasn't forgiven me for what I said about his wife. He walks like a pensioner to the bathroom, looking like he has aged overnight. I must try to avoid him or he will drag me down with him. I hear him gasp through the bathroom door, then the sound of his piss hitting the side of the bowl. He's even started to urinate like an old man, in spurts.

I do my own ablutions when he emerges, and find myself thinking about my wife –the Commander's questions have put her back in my mind. I hope she has survived the coup, not for my sake, but what would my daughter do without having that structure in her life, of visiting her mother every day, brushing her hair and turning her in the bed, and arranging her flowers?

That child. A few weeks ago she left her journal on the kitchen table. She had asked me for a recipe late at night – something basic, like how to make stock – and had scribbled it in the book and then gone to bed, leaving it closed on the table. Her journal began to call my name; it began to burn a hole in the table. I started cautiously, opening it at random and snatching bits of prose. Then I saw the page where she had listed names of men, three thick columns of them; men she had slept with. I stopped being cautious and read her journal like a book, from start to finish. In the morning she asked me what was wrong and said my face looked pinched and worn as if I'd heard that somebody had died in the night. I asked her if she had lost her self-respect and she knew immediately what I'd done. She asked me if I had enjoyed it, if I'd enjoyed the part about her trying to have sex in a swimming pool.

In the death throes of our marriage my wife and I became frantic lovers, like hospital patients with third-degree burns on an adrenaline high in response to the pain. She slept with me in the morning even when she knew I had been with someone else the night before. After so many years of marriage, and a child, her body had rebelled and turned upon itself. The women I chose to spend my nights with had all the usual attractions for a man of my age, and my wife understood this. She went crazy only after I left her – it was my daughter's boyfriend who had to knock down walls in the house.

The barber is waiting for the bathroom when I open the door. He is letting his beard bloom unchecked and has avoided speaking to me since I prepared the paella (the Commander used his finger to sop up the last juices on his plate, which thrilled me). The portraitist is eating a tomato like a piece of fruit, whole, but I don't touch my share of the bread and cheese. I'm craving fried prawn flesh, overcooked so that it begins to cream, the meat past the point of resisting. A knock on the door signals my release: it's the same guard as yesterday, still in button-down shirt and loosened tie like a banker at the office at midnight. The portraitist and barber will stay in the room today – I did without kitchen boys on Sundays in the President's apartment and I will do without them today.

We walk in silence to the kitchen, along the balconies that give onto the central courtyard. The Summer Residence is bustling like a hotel on a Friday morning. Men and women group in the courtyard, on benches and around picnic tables. I have not seen women here before. They too are in similar after-hours workwear – slacks and pencil skirts and sleeveless knitted tops, sensible shoes. One of them glances up at me and smiles, making me feel alive. I would like to add her to my album. I wonder if my house has been left intact, if the album is still on its shelf in my bedroom: in it I have a photograph of every woman I have pursued. It's the old kind, with plastic sheets over adhesive backs that have lost their glue over the years, and the photos have started to escape the plastic film holding them down, to creep off the pages. This is what old age does to a man: even past conquests want to escape you. My daughter used to beg me to get it out, to tell her the tale of each woman as a bedtime story. Bedtime stories indeed. I would tone it down for her when she was younger, make each woman the heroine of our romance, give her details about their dresses and perfumes and how they wore their hair. Later she became shrewd and probing. She wasn't content with fairytales, she wanted to know who these women really were and how I had seduced them. Her first boyfriend was regaled with tales from the album – she invited him to my place for dinner and brought out the album when I brought out the coffee. 'Tell us the stories, Dad,' she said. 'Start from the beginning.' It only strikes me now that my daughter could easily have asked if I'd lost my self-respect.

The first woman I slept with was the least attractive of them all; in the photo her knees are fat and dimpled. We skimmed over her, to get to what I like to call the model years. Two years, many models; I had just begun to grasp the power of making women feel wanted. The first woman I spotted from my car. At a red traffic light I stopped next to her and looked across, and at the next light I stopped behind her, noticed her left brake light wasn't working, wrote down her licence number, and called up the traffic department that afternoon pretending we'd had an accident so they would give me her name. I found out where she lived and sent her flowers that evening with a note attached: 'Your left brake light is broken. Call me.' Within two days we had dinner plans. In the photo she is dressed in satin for a shoot.

Much further on in the album is my wife. I decided to marry her on a Saturday evening, at a dangerous time of the day when the light was so beautiful I wanted to prostrate myself and offer a sacrifice to it. I'd taken her to an afternoon movie and came out of the theatre feeling vulnerable; afternoon movies have always done that to me, something about whiling away two hours of my life in a darkened room when it is still light outside. I drove her home but couldn't find a space right outside her apartment, so I parked further down the road and walked her to the gate, a picket fence, about knee-high, shielding a tiny garden from trespassers. I don't remember if we kissed goodbye. I had almost reached my car when I heard her shout my name; as I turned I saw her leap over the picket fence and run towards me in her boots, and when she got to me she jumped and hooked her legs about my hips and her arms behind my neck, and kissed me with such passion I decided to marry her.

I learned about sex from animals – chickens, to be precise – like most poor boys. My mother, harried, asked me to go out to the coop to get some eggs one morning when the sun was high and I was less than twelve years old. I pushed the gate open and stood in the chicken run, to discover the cock in a compromising position with a hen. I shut the gate again quickly behind me and crouched beside them in the sunlight. He paused for a while, watching me suspiciously with one lidless black eye, then reanimated himself, setting the flap of loose skin below his chin in motion. This went on until my mother screamed from inside for the eggs, but I couldn't drag myself away; his movements were mesmerizing. But it wasn't the sex that made me keep those photographs of women, in fact I've never enjoyed sex much. When we decided to have a child, my wife had to plot ways to lure me into bed more often. One afternoon I was outside mowing the lawn, shirtless, the cut grass sticking to the sweat on my back, and she called for me, promising cold lemonade. A ruse, it turned out: she was ovulating.

The ingredients I asked for are waiting for me in the kitchen, some of them still alive. The crayfish butt against the sink wall and each other in slow motion, their long limbs finding no tenure on the metal. The prawns are grey and succulent, with foetus eyes, and the sea snails have withdrawn into their shells and stoppered them against violence. A fish has already been skinned, gutted, de-boned and quartered, its flesh pearled and pink. There is garlic, eggs, butter, herbs by the bunch, mayonnaise, olive and groundnut oil, and a sack of lemons. Basic, but seafood is best with little adornment. The man takes his leave of me. The Commander has begun to trust that I will not put ground glass in his omelette.

I will start by deep-frying the fish in a pan half-full of groundnut oil. My sous-chef used to believe it was his responsibility to start with the creatures that were still alive, to put them out of their waterless misery. It was excruciating to him that abalone had to be left for hours to relax before they were ready to die. I doubt he survived the gunshot. When they dragged me out of the kitchen, he was lying face-down on the floor at the service exit, his blood around him. I cannot say that I was glad of this, but I know that he had been biting at my heels like a small, yapping dog, hoping to tire me so that he could bring me down. The President told me one Sunday morning in his apartment, through a mouthful of crabcake, that he was ready for a change. I interpreted it as a warning and the next morning in the Residence kitchens the sous-chef could smell I felt threatened. My fear of usurpation rose off me in waves and it encouraged him.

I hold a thermometer in a cup of hot water, then dip it in the oil. It is ready for the fish. I coat each fillet in flour and pepper and slip it gently into the pan; when the pieces rise to the surface I will know they are ready. I turn from the stove to attend to the prawns. The woman I noticed in the courtyard has entered silently and is standing next to the sink, watching the crayfish. She turns to me, smiling. Her pencil skirt compacts her lower body beautifully. Her arms are bare and tapered.

'Are you always this cruel?' she says.

I am stirred by her. Stirred to desire. 'They can't feel pain.

Haven't you heard of the gutted shark that took its own insides as bait?'

'I know they scream as they die in a pot of boiling water.'

'Just trapped air being released from their shells,' I respond.

She looks back down at the struggling crayfish. The fish pieces have begun to surface, browned. I take a slotted spoon and lift each one out and onto crumpled absorbent paper towel, which darkens around each oily piece. I keep my back to her, feeling watched.

'Are you here to make sure I don't poison the Commander?' I say archly.

She doesn't answer.

'It would be easy, you know. I could forget to disembowel the crayfish, undercook the fish, use opened mussels in the soup. Don't think I haven't considered it.'

Her silence persists, forcing me to turn around and look at her again. She has lifted a crayfish by the carapace and broken off its feeler; it squirms and searches the air tentatively with a pincer. She finds its anus and inserts the feeler smoothly. The creature contracts. Then she pulls it out again in one movement and the intestinal tube comes out casing the feeler. The shit is green.

'I usually wait for them to die before I do that,' I say. 'Even if they can't feel pain.'

This is true. I have never disembowelled a live crayfish.

She drops the crayfish back into the sink and soaps her hands rigorously. When she turns to face me again, I see traces of some faint disappointment.

'Did you know that crayfish have a grain of sand in their

brains that gives them their bearings?' I ask her. 'That's how they know up from down. A supplier told me he once put a metal filing in a crayfish's brain, and a magnet at the bottom of the tank, and the crayfish swam upside down until it died.'

She steps away from the sink and perches on a kitchen stool near the swinging doors, the same place the two men sat the night I made paella. Her pencil skirt forces her to cross her legs. Her ankles are slim and veined and even her closed-toe shoes can't detract from the elegance of her feet. She looks the other way, uninterested. The water is boiling, I drop the sea snails into the steaming pot, and they immediately begin to scream – at first silently, a whine so high-pitched only a dog could hear it, then descending to a moan designed for the human ear. They rattle in the pot against each other's shells and after a few minutes they give up and their stoppers first float to the top, then sink to the bottom. When I drain them they clatter into the sink – the side that was attached to the creature is smooth, with a blue copper swirl, the other side is stuccoed and prickly.

I select a sharp knife, get a grip on a stunted boiled sea snail and slice it finely. It pares off firm and grey.

'Where have all the women come from?' I ask.

She doesn't answer until I'm forced to twist my head to see if she is still in the kitchen. She has her hands above her head, twirling a sausage of hair around itself into a bun, the faint line of a muscle showing in her upper arms.

'There are new men here too,' she says. 'We've been keeping order in the city – trying to stop looting, getting services running again.'

'And now that's been achieved? Does order reign?'

She pauses and tucks a wayward hair behind her ear. 'To a degree.'

I begin to crush garlic cloves with coarse salt, pressing them with the flat of the knife against the board until they yield, then turn to paste. 'What's it like out there? What are people doing? Are houses intact?'

She laughs and stands. 'You mean, is your house intact?'

I smile conspiratorially, take a frying pan down by its handle and cover the base with oil. She walks towards me and I hand her the pan, and the garlic and sea snail on a wooden board. 'Fry this until it becomes opaque.'

She takes the handle, finds a spatula and hovers over the pan solicitously until the garlic releases its scent into the oil. 'People are confused. Many had chosen not to know about the President's crimes.'

I look at her inquisitively.

'Of course you don't know,' she says. 'Convenient.'

I notice small pieces of grass clinging to her back and flecking her hair. She must have been lying outside in the sun this morning.

I have the rolling pin in my hand – it is time to creep up on the abalone and surprise them with a death blow. She watches me walk the length of the kitchen towards the darkened pantry; I tiptoe the last few steps for dramatic effect and then crouch above them. Three I kill before they contract, but the last realizes what is coming and stiffens. I will have to throw it out.

She looks at me carrying my spoils back to the sink and says, 'Death by rolling pin. Must remember that one.'

I fry the three steaks quickly, searing their flanks. She dries her hands on a dishcloth and leans against the sink, facing me. The prawns have pinkened in hot oil.

'Will you put your disembowelled friend and his companions out of their misery?' I ask her.

She looks sheepish as she lifts each one and drops it into the pot. The one missing a feeler has died in the sink. They begin to scream. 'Did the man who kept watch on you before ever help you cook?' she asks.

'He never offered.'

'Neither did I.'

'You had blood on your hands. You couldn't refuse.'

'Crayfish shit. Not blood.'

I reach for her hand across the pot. She lets me hold it briefly, then pulls her arm back.

'The steam. It's burning me.'

I notice neat circles of discoloured flesh on the inside of her forearm. Six small circles in a row, the skin creased and stretched.

Behind me, a man clears his throat – the Commander. He is standing just inside the kitchen, next to the pantry. Does it matter if he saw? His beauty makes me feel ashamed and I look down at my hands, the hands of an old man – too many years of using them to make my living. She has turned to wash her hands in the sink again. The Commander approaches, picks a prawn from the oil and dangles it, waiting for it to cool, then peels the prawn with one hand, removes the head and chews.

He reaches out his hand to her, 'Come, darling, let us seat ourselves.'

They leave through the swinging doors, her arm through his. I take off my apron and hat and carry through two platters and a plate of cut lemons. He immediately sets about using his long fingers, dipping bits of flesh into a pot of melted butter, squeezing lemon with gusto, de-shelling and digging for the most succulent bits of the creatures. I hunch at the kitchen counter and chew on a few secretly hoarded cooked prawns. They are as I wanted – creamed past the point of resistance.

9 *His barber*

The portraitist has asked the man who brought us bread and tomatoes if we can go for a walk in the courtyard. Why he wants to walk is beyond me since he has been struggling just to get to the bathroom and back and when he stands from sitting, he keeps one hand on his belly and uses the other, palm spread, to support his lower back like a pregnant woman. The man surprised us by agreeing, but he said he'd follow behind us a few metres, keep an eye on us. The chef has scuttled off sideways like a scavenger to attend to his crustaceans.

My pyjamas cleave to me like a second skin, filthy, and my beard is encroaching on virgin territory. We leave the room like an old married couple going to church, the man trailing us at an uninterested distance. The portraitist shuffles along the corridor next to me.

'What is it?' I ask him. 'Why are you walking like that?'

He looks at me as if he's surprised I noticed. 'Lower back. Must have pinched a nerve in my sleep.'

'There are exercises you can do, you know – to release it. I'll show you back in the room.'

We turn the corner into the passage that opens onto the courtyard below. It is full of people. We lean on the railing and look down at the tops of their heads; many of them are women, sitting in small groups, bucolic in the late morning light.

'Party officials,' the man who has been trailing us says. 'They arrived last night.'

He has joined us at the railing, and leans a little too far out over his arms, ogling the women. The portraitist, too, stares at each woman like a hungry man. At first I wonder that his eye could be roving so soon, but then I realize that he is only staring in the hope that one of them will be his wife. No wonder he was so desperate to get out of the room – he wants to find her, or see her, or glimpse her. I turn my eyes back down to the courtyard. Something is not right: I find that each person I look at seems to jolt some recollection in my mind, to reignite some memory pathway.

'Every person I see looks vaguely familiar,' I say to the portraitist softly. 'Should that worry me?'

'In a strange place, your brain does things like that,' he says. 'Seeks out familiarity. A survival tactic.'

Perhaps. I have almost accepted his explanation when I see her – not vaguely familiar, but intimately known: my brother's fiancée, who disappeared when he did. She is sitting on the grass in the sun, her face offered up to it like a sacrifice, with her closed-toe shoes kicked off and her pencil skirt keeping her legs chastely together, crossed at the ankles, toes curled as she soaks up the warmth. That thick hair. I used to find strands of it on my brother's pillow when I was younger, so young that I would snoop about his room, desperate for clues about things older boys did, for clues about women, and sex, and intimacy. I collected what she had left behind, the only evidence she had been there, thick enough that even singly I could tie them into knots without snapping them. I couldn't believe those hairs were dead.

She opens her eyes and the angle her face makes with the sun means she is looking directly at me. Do I flatter myself to think she would recognize me? That she has banked my face in her memory? She closes her eyes again, uncrosses her ankles and lies down completely, her head against her palms, relaxed.

'I just want to see her,' says the portraitist. 'Not even speak to her or touch her, I just want to see her.'

His wife. The man guarding us, in the intimacy that comes from looking at women together, says, 'She walks in the rose garden in the mornings, on the other side of the courtyard. We let her walk and stretch for an hour.'

The portraitist grips his forearm. 'I have to see her. Please. She doesn't even need to know I'm there.'

The man is feeling good in the sun. Maybe he has his own lover amongst the women milling below. He hesitates, then agrees. 'You can see the rose garden from the opposite passageway. I'll take you there.' He turns to me. 'I'll watch you from across the courtyard. I know you won't move.'

I won't move. She is beneath me, in the sun. An image of my mother flits into my mind like a fly that needs swatting: in the hospital, disguised by tubes, thinking I was my brother and crying with joy that he had found her at last. Her last words were: 'My son', but she wasn't speaking about me.

I say my brother's fiancée's name, then call it more loudly, and a few people in the courtyard look up at me, registering my presence. I shout it and she opens her eyes and sits up, looking around her to source the voice. A man points up to me, to the railing where I'm standing, and she looks up, shielding her face from the sun with one hand. She can't see me because of the glare. She stands and walks barefoot towards the edge of the courtyard and looks up, then disappears from my sight, into the passageway beneath me. I am relieved, relieved that it isn't her, that I don't need to know. Somebody touches my shoulder gently and I turn. It's her. She stands before me, barefoot on the cement floor, her hair ruffled from lying on the grass, slightly out of breath from running up the stairs.

'My God,' she whispers. 'For a moment I thought…'

I know what she is thinking, she and my mother, wishing me away, wishing he were back.

She reaches out a long limb to cup my face. 'With that beard…' She can't finish the sentence. She doesn't need to. 'What are you doing here? Are you with the movement? What section are you in?' She is holding back tears unsuccessfully; they bank and spill, bank and spill.

'I'm being held captive. I was taken in during the coup. They're keeping me with two other men in a room.'

'Captive?' She wipes her tears away impatiently, trying to concentrate on my words. 'But that's impossible, there must be a mistake…'

'No mistake. I'm one of the old guard. I shaved him each day, plucked hair from his nose, made him look presentable…'

'The President?' she says, incredulously.

'The President.'

'You mean you held a knife to his throat every day and never slit it?' Her tears begin to collect again. 'After what he did? To me, to your brother?' They are spilling hopelessly now. Her face is blotched with the effort of her grief.

45

I am beginning to resent her accusations. 'What *did* he do to my brother?'

She has covered her face with two hands, blocking me out and everything I recall in her.

'What happened to him?'

She moves her hands, holds them out to me, to take my hands in hers. I relent, and she holds them, rubbing them with her thumbs, looking at me with pity. 'You don't know, do you?' she whispers. 'Of course you don't. Why does nobody *know*?'

She pulls me towards her, nestles her head against my chest. I am taller than her, but only just, and she has to stoop slightly. Then she pushes me away as suddenly as she drew me to her, and steps away from me, remembering some forgotten propriety. She looks around us, looks down at her bare feet, feels with her hand for her collapsed hairbun. Fraternizing with the enemy. She glances over the railing, down at the people grouped below. Nobody is paying us any attention. She looks over her shoulder, her neck tendons diagonal for a second, as if expecting somebody to be lurking, eavesdropping behind the columns of the passageway, then she rubs the inside of her right arm compulsively. Whom is she conjuring?

'He died in the mountains,' she says quietly. 'We were ambushed. We left the village to make a difference, to change things.' She looks over her shoulder again, keeping her distance from me impersonal. She opens her mouth, takes a breath to relaunch.

I have to interrupt. 'I know he's dead,' I say, trying to keep my bile masked. 'I got the letter. I suppose you saw him being buried.'

She burns at this, catches alight like a holy bush in the desert. 'So you did know.' Then she turns her back to me, lifts her hands to recoil her hair, and says softly, 'Traitor.'

She walks down the stairs, pointing each graceful foot before it lands. I watch her ease onto the courtyard grass, pick up her shoes with one hand, and merge with the shade boxing in the sunswept courtyard.

10 *His portraitist*

'There she is,' the man says, and pulls me behind a pillar so I'm not exposed.

She is walking as fast as our child will let her around the small rose garden, forced by the narrow path to turn comically often. From this level, I can see her full head of hair from above, her parting straight until halfway back her skull where it veers sideways. The grey strands have gathered courage and refuse to be flattened into a ponytail; she doesn't have her hair dye as an ally anymore. On Saturday mornings she used to look like a mad surgeon, emerging from the bathroom with two plastic gloves held up as if she were waiting for a nurse to remove them, and a showercap covering her hair, the dye coaxing the plastic red against its will. If she were careless, the rims of her ears would be slightly pink for days.

To give birth in captivity. If I think too long about the position I've put her in, my mind begins to seize up like a crushed windpipe. She looks fine – healthy and vigorous – but what is the stress doing to our child, unseen? Coursing through her into the baby, a fatal kind of nourishment. Will they let us go once she has had the child? Why are they even keeping me here, insignificant player that I am? Why has he dragged me into this cycle of confession and witnessing? Stop. Stop it.

My kidneys pulse in response; they have a muscle memory of their own.

She has done another abrupt turn and is pumping her arms, propelling herself forwards, eyes level, face determined. Her breasts bob slightly from the motion, getting in the way of her arms on every backward swing. She stops and bends to touch her toes, stretches sideways, lifts her arms in the air. What would we be doing right now if none of this had happened? She would be sitting in the sun after her bath, topless, rubbing lemon juice onto her nipples – she said this prepared them for the onslaught of breastfeeding – the small potted palms on our balcony keeping this a secret from the street. I would be in my dressing gown in my studio, music blaring, working on a drawing I was planning to give her after the birth – charcoal, like the ones she'd originally admired at my exhibition. She used to wander around the kitchen with just a sarong tied around her waist and faint traces of lemon pulp and sometimes a stray pip sticking to her breasts. Our fridge was stocked with champagne and each time I opened the rattling door it felt like a mini-celebration just from the sight of the gold foil and green glass; this was in case her milk didn't come quickly enough after the birth – she said a few sips of champagne would get it flowing.

Now she is lying on the grass between the gravel, lifting each leg slowly in the air and holding it in the stretch. She looks like just another stone sculpture planted in the surrounding garden – conventional shapes: cupids, half-naked women, tentative sprites. The rigidity of the sculptures reminds me of a boy I saw on the beach when I was young enough not yet to have chosen a profession. He was on his hands and knees in the sand, sculpting life-sized sand creatures – buffalo, crocodiles, lions, giant tortoises – his only tool an old detergent bottle filled with sea water. He sprayed the sand and then used his hands to mould animals so realistic they scared me; it was as if they had bones and muscles and sinews and were waiting for the sun to set so that they could stand and stretch and begin to hunt. He had no pictures with him; the animals were entirely in his mind's eye. I sat and watched him until the light was gone and I could no longer see, further down the beach, obedient swimmers swarming in a thick triangle between the flags. Choosing to be an artist never seemed like a risky thing to do; in fact, it seemed to be a guarantee against risk.

A soft voice with fishy breath speaks into my left ear: 'The child is getting impatient. It wants to greet the world, meet its father. She's looking well, no?'

I turn to look at the Commander. He is picking his teeth with a twig, working away at something caught in the gum next to his incisor. He keeps his eyes fixed on my wife. She is still on her back in the grass, leg pulled towards her in a stretch, and I wish she would stand up, get out of that ridiculous position.

'Quite a catch,' he says. 'Don't know what she saw in him.'

'In me?'

'Yes, in you.'

'Thank you.'

He laughs. Then he calls out my wife's name and she looks up, suspicious. 'Darling, we have your husband here to see you. Can you bear to look at him?'

The Commander pulls me from behind the pillar like a schoolroom dunce. I stand at the railing awkwardly, not knowing what to do with my hands. She looks up at me patiently, with forbearance. Putting up with me. Is that what she's doing?

'Hello,' she says, her voice raised so that it will reach me. 'How are you?'

How am I? My God, how am I?

'Fine.' I put my hands on the railings. 'And you?'

'OK.' She puts one hand on her hip.

'And the baby…?' I ask.

She puts her other hand on her stomach. 'Alive and kicking.' She glances at the Commander as she says this.

I look at him too. He is smiling down at her like a priest from a pulpit. I suddenly feel desperate to connect with her, to know if she forgives me, to hear her say she loves me, and for this I will even risk humiliation. Her face is as smooth and impenetrable as an egg. This deliberate obtuseness used to bring me pleasure, when I could still take for granted that she would be sleeping beside me each night, and could guess at her emotions as if it were a game. Now her shield is unbearable and I would do anything to crack it and see through to her heart.

'Do you hate me?' I say to her, my voice quavering. 'Do you hate me for what I've done?'

'You forget it was my father who got you the job,' she says drily.

The Commander laughs.

'I love you,' I say to her, the panic rising.

Am I imagining that her face becomes tender for an instant, that she closes her eyes to stop tears? She looks up at me and then the baby kicks and the shock of its movement flits across her face. She puts her other hand on her belly too, and looks down at the unborn child, so insistent.

'Stop it,' she says to me. 'Stop doing this.' She turns and walks through the rose garden back into the Summer Residence, without looking back.

I slump onto the railing, fighting back tears.

'Her father got you the job?' the Commander says slyly.

'I don't suppose I have the choice not to answer your questions.'

'No, you don't. How did it happen?'

He takes me by the arm like an invalid and starts to walk me down the passage. I try to disguise my shuffle, but he picks it up and slows his steps to suit mine.

'He pulled some strings. I was hired to paint the President's family.'

'Did she try to seduce you?'

'Who?'

'The President's wife.'

'Yes. He knew about it. She was too old for his liking by then anyway. He preferred younger stock.'

'Like your wife.'

'My wife?'

'Somebody of her age.'

'Well, yes, I suppose…'

'Did you fall for her?'

'For who?'

'For the President's wife.'

'Of course not. I loved my wife. I love my wife.'

'So she was too old for your liking too.'

'That's not the point.'

We turn a corner in the passageway and find the barber leaning heavily on the railings, staring down into the courtyard.

The Commander offers him his other arm. The barber looks at the man trailing behind us a few steps, decides it's not worth making a fuss, and reluctantly lets the Commander hook his arm beneath his. He stands, rigid, willing himself not to be repulsed. We continue on our walk, a stiff three-legged race in slow motion, until we arrive at our bedroom door.

The Commander turns to me. 'I'd like you to start tomorrow on a portrait. And you'll cut my hair tomorrow afternoon,' he says to the barber. He drops our arms suddenly like two sacks of flour he has carried as a burden and walks briskly away.

'Come,' says the barber from inside the room. 'I'll show you how to unpinch that nerve.'

I close the door behind me.

'Lie down – no, on the floor, not your bed. You need a hard surface for this to work.'

I ease myself slowly towards the floorboards. He stands above me, his beard an upside-down halo.

'Now bend your right leg and pull it across your left leg. You should hear your spine click.'

I wish it were that simple. He is young, this barber, and optimistic. He must be in his late twenties. I haven't asked him anything about his life; all three of us have been in siege mode, thinking only of our own survival, unwilling to form a bond that might implicate us further. My mind has been full of my wife, my own pain.

'There – did you hear it?' he says hopefully. My back has clicked despite itself. 'Now pull your knees to your chest and rock your spine against the floor, like a cradle.'

I obey him, even though this movement forces my kidneys

into impossible contortions. He sees me wince. I lie still on the floor, my legs extended.

'Do you have family you left behind?' I ask him.

He sits on the bed, his legs dangling, and says nothing.

I get to my feet and hobble to my own bed. 'I haven't asked you whether there's a wife or child waiting for you when you get out.'

'No,' he says. 'I'm not married. My mother died last year.'

'Siblings?'

'I had a brother. Died years ago.'

'Does anybody know you've been taken?'

'My shop assistant must have figured out something happened. But if there's been a coup nobody will be worrying about anybody but themselves.'

I get a sudden glimpse into what it must be like for the Commander, with people not knowing anything, not knowing what was done in the President's name.

'He did awful things, you know,' I can't resist saying.

The barber is silent, so I lift my head to look at him. He removes his shoes and socks and slowly lies down on the bed, on his hip, facing me.

'Who did?' he says.

'The President.'

'How awful?' he says. 'What did he do?' I can't decipher his tone.

'Had people killed. Dissidents. That sort of thing.' I dare not go any further.

'You knew this and kept working for him?' He looks at me quizzically.

'No…' Now look what I've done. I'll have to tell him more. 'The Commander told me.'

'And you believe him? How do you know he's telling the truth?'

'Photographs. He has photographs. Of people who were killed.'

The barber swings his legs off the bed and goes to the window. The curtains are half-closed, but he sweeps them open vigorously. The valley below is hazy in the midday light, expectant, waiting for evening and the promise of shadows. From the way his back is tensed, I assume our conversation is over, so I roll onto my stomach and try to sleep. Something that the Commander said to me has been percolating in my brain. About the President's wife. Of course she told her husband, that I understand. They must have laughed about it, lying in their twin beds in the first-floor bedroom, about how she'd seduced the gangly artist, the young portraitist, persuaded him to sleep with her. But why would the President tell the Commander something like that?

The President's wife was suffocating to look at – her pores were so blocked from years of foundation use I always wondered how her skin could still breathe. It happened on the third night of my stay at the Summer Residence. She had been sitting for me for two days, with pearls strung around her neck and a gold pendant that kept getting stuck between her sweating breasts each time she shifted. Mock-coy, she would dislodge it slowly as if we were sharing a secret, and I would turn my attention furiously to my palette. The President watched us that afternoon, sitting behind me on a small chair upholstered with velvet. She made eyes at me even more vigorously as a result.

At dinner, the four of us – my wife was there too – sat with our plates on our laps on the deck overlooking the sea. They were redecorating the house so there was no picnic table for eating outside, and it was too hot to sit indoors. We served ourselves in the dining room and then carried out our plates and perched on the edge of our chairs, sitting in a row facing the sea, which made conversation difficult. Whenever the President said something, I tried to turn my head to face him, but his wife was sitting between us and she obstinately kept her head right in front of his. It was a meal full of discomfort, of making sure I hadn't left food on my face, of wanting to take a second helping but worrying it would look gluttonous. I remember trying to keep my elbows tucked against my sides while eating a chicken drumstick without cutlery. My wife dropped her fork on the deck and went to fetch another from inside.

The President said, his mouth full of coleslaw, 'We'd like you to keep going on the portrait tonight. You seem to be making good progress. My wife would like to keep working.'

I craned my neck to see his face, but her head was still in the way, her thick nostrils quivering like a giant trying to smell her prey. She chewed on a piece of meat, her mouth primly closed until she swallowed, then parted her lips and said, 'It would be a pity for us to lose momentum.' My wife resettled herself on her chair with a clean fork.

We had already been trying for a child for over a year at that stage. Sex had become a trial for me, only a few years into our marriage. My wife would remove her underwear to shower in the morning and curse when she discovered the first smudge of her period. I would lie on the bed, watching her through the haze of just-departed sleep, and feel personally responsible. We stopped making love at any time other than when she was ovulating, and then it felt clinical, like a doctor doing something to a patient. When she finally did fall pregnant, she took all the credit. I don't blame her, of course. I did want a child, but more as living proof of my complete union with her, than for the child itself. I was afraid – perhaps I still am – that I would be left out when it arrived, that all her love and attention would be redirected to this child, and I would be left holding the toys and the baby bag full of clean nappies and bottles, alone. She seemed possessive of the child, even before it could be called a child – when it was the size of a grain of rice – and wouldn't let me put my ear to her belly to hear its heartbeat.

When we had finished eating that evening, the President's wife went to her bedroom to prepare, and I kissed my wife and left her with the President out on the deck. A night wind had come up, full of sea salt, and her hair was being whipped around her head like a helicopter blade. She smiled at me strangely, as if she knew something I didn't. I turned to look back at her from the dining room, through the glass of the sliding door, and saw she'd taken out her pocket mirror and was applying lipstick, flicking her hair out of her face and mouth repeatedly. The President watched her from his deckchair, mesmerized. I was used to seeing men look at her like that, but that time it made a thirst well up in me, a crippling nostalgia for the simple days of our courtship when she hadn't yet come to equate marriage, and me, with disappointment.

I walked barefoot through the dimly lit house to the studio, the plush pile giving way beneath my feet. The studio was the only room built into the roof and doubled as a kind of observatory, with a domed glass ceiling and a telescope pointed at Saturn. I hadn't been into the studio at night before – it was beautifully lit with small lamps that glowed back at themselves in the glass, but horribly impractical for my purposes. I searched unsuccessfully for a light switch at the door for overhead lighting, then hooked my thumb into my palette and began to squeeze out small amounts of paint from the tubes I had already laid out for the next day's work.

I heard the door behind me open and shut, and twisted to see the President's wife turn the key in the lock.

'So we won't be disturbed,' she said when she saw me looking at her with my eyebrows raised. She was wearing black slacks and an off-the-shoulder jersey with beads sewn along the neckline. 'I thought we could try something a little different,' she said. 'I've always admired your drawings; I saw some years ago at an exhibition – they were sketches of your wife I believe? In pencil? Could you do something like that of me?'

Those were done before she was my wife, when it aroused her to be under my gaze as it wavered between that of lover and of artist. She would strip silently in my bedroom and then walk naked to the tiny, cramped kitchen that doubled as my studio and perch on a stool with her back to me, inviting me to draw.

'Let's start with something simple,' the President's wife said. 'What if I sit on this chair facing forwards?'

And then in one movement she pulled her jersey over her head and stood before me, her hair slightly static and her breasts still marked from the wiring of her bra. I'm not sure what it was that made me sleep with her in the end. The thrill of being desired? Payback for the way my wife had applied lipstick in my wake? Perhaps it was just that she stirred pity in me and desire surprised me by stirring with it. The zip on her slacks caught on her underwear and for a few seconds she was bent over, her breasts lunging towards the floor, trying to unhook them. She blushed then, a blush so profound it showed even through her foundation. And I pitied her.

I flip onto my back, my brainwork heating up the pillow. Of course. The President's wife is being kept here too. Why else would the President call out her name in the loneliness of his pain? If I was close to power, she was closer.

11 *His chef*

I have just remembered that I left a pocket of potatoes, skinned and halved, on the cutting board in the kitchen. I forgot to transfer them to a tub of water and tonight they will be green from being left in the air too long. I take a chair out to the balcony and put my legs up on the railings. It is only early afternoon, but the light is already starting to magnify the colour in the valley below.

This woman, the Commander's wife, is making me feel like a boy trapped in an old man's body: desire inflames my loins, but with no visible result. She let me hold her hand in the kitchen, briefly, until the steam from the pot singed her arm and the Commander surprised us, but I know he doesn't mind. He reminds me of myself at his age; I would catch strangers staring at me in a movie queue or at the bank – they always looked like they were trying to drink in my beauty, to ingest it and make it their own. In bed, women would tell me they wanted to possess me. There was one woman – a doctor – who thought beauty was the elixir of life, and she latched onto me and sucked away until I cast her off. But it never bothered me if I caught one of my women with another man, even my wife.

My daughter's face and my own are unnervingly similar. Male beauty does not translate well to a female; she has a hardness about her jaw and I always half-expect to find stubble pushing its way through her pores. But she still attracts men, especially the ones who don't know what they want. My own rule was to treat women like stations on a radio: if you listen to one for too long, who knows what you're missing on the next bandwidth? The cloying ones fell to pieces, of course. And my wife did too, in the end.

There is a shifting in the low shrubs beneath the balcony and the Commander's wife emerges from the overgrown path, her eyes already raised to my level. Was she looking for me? My old heart wants to believe it. She has changed out of her uniform and now wears a summer dress that pulls slightly over her hips, and her hair has been released from its coil. She smiles at me with restraint and calls, 'What's for dinner?' I stand and lean on the balcony, glad that I'd unbuttoned the top three buttons of my shirt before she arrived.

'I'm making pastry at four in the morning, while it's still cool enough for the butter to stay firm. Care to join me?'

She reaches down to fix her sandal strap and when she lifts her head again her smile fades beneath my gaze – she is looking at something behind me. I turn and see the barber standing in the doorway, looking down at her with sleep still rising warmly from his head. He comes forward and leans on the rail next to me.

She pulls at her dress where it clings and looks at him. 'I'm sorry,' she says. 'I had no right.'

He rubs the back of his head and clears his throat. 'But perhaps you do.' He glances at me as if I'm eavesdropping.

I look back at him obstinately, my arms firmly on the rail, but she looks at me imploringly until I sigh loudly and walk back into the room, a word flitting around in my head: cuckolded. Cuckolded. I sit on my bed facing the window and see the barber, really see him, for the first time. He's dark and vital, with veins that expose the strength of his blood and hair that flows from his head like the fountain of youth itself. But there's something crumpled about him, about the way he walks and the sound of his voice, as if he'd been crushed when he was small and never recovered. He reminds me of my daughter, that's what it is – it makes me want to reach out to him and to despise him at the same time.

It's silent on the balcony – what kind of game are these two playing? I lean sideways and peer around the open door. He is holding an apple with a note tied around it with masking tape, greedily ripping the tape with his teeth to release the note from its fruity prison. Ingenious. And what would the Commander think about all this? The barber reads it quickly, then nods agreement to her. I listen to her sandals click against her feet as she walks away. Such small things can summon desire.

My fingers smell of garlic and coriander, years' worth of the stuff. The barber comes inside.

'Lucky boy,' I say to him. 'Midnight tryst planned? Well done.'

He ignores me. It's hard to think of myself as an old man. My daughter said that to me the day before I was brought in here. 'You're an old man,' she said. 'You will die soon. I don't know if I will miss you.' People don't realize what it's like to age when you're beautiful, to feel like you reached your peak when you turned forty and every day since that day you've become just a small bit uglier. A less attractive man has nothing to lose when he ages. As an older man, I am still handsome, but there is an invisible line that I've crossed: my body's done a dirty deal with gravity and my hair has given up the ghost once and for all. It's not the wrinkles, it's things you're never told to expect – having to piss five times a night, discovering that your calf muscles are disintegrating against your will, leaving you bandy-legged, watching the spider veins cast their purple webs across the backs of your knees, waking up with your eyelids sealed together because your eyes can no longer self-lubricate. And now this: desire that exists without proof. All this shutting down must have a purpose. I think what my daughter was implying is that it's meant to encourage reckoning and accounting. Moral reckoning.

OK then, let's reckon. I don't believe my wife was ever really mad. I think mental illness is a luxury most people can't afford. Even after her psychiatrist had persuaded me to put her in an institution, I would sneak into the gardens and look through the window into her room on the ground floor, always half-expecting to catch her doing something that would prove she was pretending. I never really thought about what that something would be – maybe she would be on the phone to our daughter, laughing and chatting normally? Or she would be doing yoga in her striped legwarmers, on her mat on the floor, with sweat beading gently at her hairline, and her face focused and calm? The disappointment each time I found her sleeping in her bed or staring at the television or sitting on the low armchair rubbing her hands would start deep in my gut and work its way up to the back of my throat where it gagged me.

Having been failed by my own flesh, and those of my flesh,

what else can an old man turn to except power to shore himself up, or at least proximity to power? We all know power and desire couple effortlessly.

12 *His barber*

She had tucked the key beneath the tape around the apple when she threw it up to me on the balcony. A poison-green apple, like the kind we used to grow in the back garden of my mother's house. She remembers them, of course. It was a small miracle that anything could push its way through that ground, so sandy it couldn't be called soil. The fruit always tasted salty; perhaps the water table had been contaminated by sea water. There was a mulberry bush in the back too, a thriving plant that unfurled leaves textured like the surface of a brain, and my brother and I fed those to his silkworms until he swapped the worms for marbles with a boy at school. We would dare each other to put a worm on our tongue and see who could bear the soft, blind wriggling the longest – once he swallowed one by accident and examined his stool meticulously the next day to see if it would emerge alive. He cut out small shapes from cardboard – stars, hearts, circles – and put them in the silkworm box that he'd punched repeatedly with a knitting needle so that the worms could breathe; slowly they spun according to his demands, desperate for something to attach their silk to, and then he hung these silken shapes from a mobile above his bed. If he gave them beetroot leaves they spun dark-pink thread instead.

I have the key hotly in my hand beneath the covers. I know

the chef intended to stay awake to watch me, but his age got the better of him, and now he is snoring on his back like a pensioner, tempting flies. I wait for her signal, straining my ears, but all I can hear are the cicadas outside lamenting the lost heat of the day, until above their scratchy chorus a single bird-note rises, sweet and clear – it's her. Within seconds I am at the door trying to coax the key noiselessly into its slot. Then I am outside in the dark, guardless corridor (who knows what she said to him?), using the wall to keep my bearings as I run down the three flights of steps to the courtyard, and there I find the door that she said would lead to the outer garden, and it does, and she stands before me in the dark, her hair gleaming, and takes my hand. I know I look like my brother right now, in the half-light, with my hair grown out and a thickly sprouted beard. An impostor.

She leads me with quiet urgency through the garden, beneath a willow tree and around a batch of strange sculptures, to a car parked on an overgrown road that seems to lead nowhere. She pops the boot of the car and motions for me to get into it. Fear flits through me until I dismiss it, but once I'm curled in the darkness like a foetus it starts to course through me violently, and I think, why did I believe her? She thinks I'm a traitor, that I'm being kept here because of my loyalty to the President. The engine hums in time to my mind's frenzy, then the car stops and I begin to imagine all the ways I could die, and I pray that the metal above my head does not pop open and betray me.

She drives on, stopping again a few minutes later. The boot hinge squeals open. 'Sorry,' she says. 'But that gate is guarded. You can sit in the front now.'

Looking up at her, at this woman whom I have just imagined

killing me in all the ways my mind would let me, I want to be a child again, and I wish it were my mother hovering above me, about to put her cool, dry hand to my forehead and tell me I'm dreaming. I try to uncurl my legs to sit up, and for a panicked second I think I'm paralysed; then my legs obey and I sit up and hook them over the edge of the open boot and propel myself to the ground. We are on a dirt road, not far from the Summer Residence – I can see it lit up in the distance like a luxury ship at sea. I want to savour this, to think of it as freedom, but the adrenaline is still pumping too fiercely through my veins and I sit in the front seat uneasily, my legs twitching with pins and needles. The road slopes down towards the vineyards in the valley below, a twisted road that seems hazardous at night. The window is open and as we descend we drive through pockets of warm air trapped from the day's heat, and emerge from them into cool air fragrant from the midnight opening of buds.

'You'll have to go back,' she says quietly, her eyes on the road. 'This is just so we can talk. I don't have the physical strength to stop you from running, but he'll find you again anyway, and then you won't be kept in a room with white linen and silver fixtures.'

I suspected this, and perhaps it's why I'm not breathing this night air with as much relish as a free man should. She doesn't speak again until we're at the base of the valley and the gnarled stumps of the vineyards are silhouetted on either side of the road like paper cut-outs of dwarves linking arms.

'Your mother…' she says.

I wait for a few seconds. 'She died last year.'

The shape of an unlit farmhouse looms ahead of us.

'She blamed me, didn't she?' she says softly. 'For what happened to your brother.'

I laugh, my voice brittle. 'No, actually. She blamed me.'

She stops the car next to the farmhouse, rests her head on the steering wheel for a few moments, then leaves the car. She is still wearing her summer dress; I can see the hem faintly beneath her coat as she walks towards the house. Her calf muscles ball and stretch as she climbs the steps onto the veranda, then she pushes tentatively at the door and disappears inside.

By the time I reach the veranda, she has re-emerged holding an unlabelled bottle of wine by its neck and a slim door wedge.

'Think you can open this?' she says, handing both to me.

I put them down on the wooden deck, push against the flyscreen and wait for my eyes to make sense of the dark room: there are barrels stacked against the wall and a tasting counter with wine bottles of increasing size, like Russian dolls that fit inside each other, arranged in a straight line. The spitting bucket is half-full and there are glasses with dirty rims – people must have left the farm in a hurry. I take two glasses and rub the rims and inner bellies with my shirt, then I fumble in the dark behind the counter and find a corkscrew next to a coil of foil shed by an already opened bottle. I take them out to the veranda, where she has pulled two cushionless deckchairs together. The cork crumbles as I twist it, and I have to push it into the bottle to clear the neck.

'There'll be bits of cork in it,' I say as I pass her a glass. 'Maybe I should have used the wedge.'

She smiles and takes the glass by the stem. The wine is warm, red, gritty. I haven't eaten since the soup we were given at four, and I feel the wine winding its hot path to my stomach.

'Do you remember my father?' she says. 'You met him at the dock. He was on a fishing crew too, not the same as your brother's. He and his twin sister were swimming in the surf when they were little, no older than ten, only chest-deep, when she was dragged out to sea by the current. He never came to terms with why he had been spared. He was sent to school the next day as if nothing had happened.'

She drains her glass and holds it out to be refilled. I pour for her, fill her glass almost to the top.

'Is that how you feel? Guilty?' she says, pulling her legs up to her chest.

'My brother chose to put himself in harm's way,' I respond.

'Your mother didn't see it like that.'

I refill my own glass. 'He was her first. She cherished him.'

'And you?'

'She remembered my brother as a golden child. Everything I did seemed dull and heavy to her.'

She holds out her glass again and smiles sheepishly, keeping her lips together – her teeth are porous and always blacken from wine; I know that from watching her drink in the kitchen with my brother when they were supposed to be babysitting me. When I hand her glass back to her she takes my hand and threads her fingers through mine. With my free hand I drink straight from the bottle.

It must be eerie for her to see me as I am now, a grown man who looks like her dead lover. The last time she saw me I was still disguised by youth, had not yet found my proper form and face, had not yet realized my genes. I think of my uncle whose wife died when their daughter was only a baby. He had adored his wife, loved her absolutely, and then suddenly her liver packed in and he was left with the small child as his only reminder of her. As she grew older she began to look uncannily like her mother, and he found himself staring at her across the supper table, watching this girl become a long-dead woman in measurable stages before his eyes. It drove him crazy in the end; he began to think she had returned to him, and that he was twenty again and courting her.

She whispers to me, tightening her hold on my hand. 'Would you sit beside me?'

I obey and she lies on her hip next to me and curls one leg across my stomach. I can feel the plastic slats of the deckchair cutting into my back; they must be cutting into her soft sides too. I lift her onto me, put my arms around the dent of her lower back to stop her from rolling off, stroke the inside of her arm, the soft skin that the sun never sees. The skin is puckered, and I hold it up to my eyes to understand it: six circles vie for space on her skin – an old scar, but not old enough to be from childhood.

'Kiss them,' she says into my ear. 'Like he used to. When the wounds were fresh.'

I kiss each circle in turn and the silken circles of my brother's mobiles flash into my mind and then are gone. She is lucky to have escaped with so few scars. She sits on me, grips my hair, digs her fingers into my beard, strokes the soft skin on my chest – all the tactile markers that remind her of him. I feel I have no choice but to let her use my body like this, to give her one more night with him. I think of my mother dying in the hospital bed with its labelled linen, saying that I mustn't speak, that I must just sit next to her with my long hair and my man's body, looking like him. There is no relief when I pull out of her on the deckchair and she falls forward onto me, sobbing, her tears running into my ears and collecting there warmly. She cries until sleep comes.

I wanted to work for the President, for the man who had killed my brother. I wanted to find a way to work for him so closely I could touch him daily, could have him briefly in my power. It wasn't difficult for me to move to the city once my mother began her descent – she hardly noticed when I kissed her goodbye. We had become outsiders at the coast by that stage anyway; the crews never forgot what my brother had done and still couldn't understand it. They thought it was frivolous to care about politics if you're putting your body on the line every day at sea. Nobody asked me to take his place on the trawler when I came of age. So I took an early bus into the city with my suitcase tied to the rack on top amidst chickens and pockets of oranges and wooden rocking chairs and anything else that somebody was going to try to sell in the city.

The first job I found in the city was disinfecting implements and sweeping hair in a salon in the Presidential District. The barber gave me a small room to stay in above the shop, with a door out onto the roof from where I could see the Residence lit up at night. The President's motorcade would regularly push itself through the narrow road the shop was on – seven black, shiny sharks in an unnatural school, none of them betraying the contents of their bellies. My guess was that the President always rode in the first one, unable to relinquish precedence even for his safety.

One afternoon, as the motorcade was passing, I asked my

boss who cut the President's hair. He was smug and amused by the question, and answered, 'I do, of course. He only takes the best.' And there it was: the chance to be close to the President, to put my hands on him. The barber went up to the Residence whenever he was bidden, which was every day, as I discovered. I had seen him leave the shop each day, for a few hours, but had not bothered to wonder about it because it was to my advantage. I used that time to practise on customers – to spray and cut and lather and shave. He didn't mind; in fact, he encouraged it because it freed him to do his presidential duty.

What makes a barber better than all other barbers? I thought about this in the evenings, sitting on the roof looking up at the Residence, wrapped in a blanket, feeling my ambition burn in my gut. I could sense it there, like a living creature, crouched and focused. I was grateful sometimes for that dogged sense of purpose that kept me calm in a strange city in the confusion of youth. During the days in the shop, I would examine each man's reactions to my movements. They would sit before me in the red swivel chair with its adjustable height lever, some looking businesslike, some looking sheepish. Many knew exactly what they wanted, many didn't, but they didn't expect pleasure, and that's what I gave them – small, almost unnoticeable pleasures that they didn't have to feel ashamed about receiving. I would brush my hand slightly against their necks as I fastened the cloth sheet; I would hold their jaws firmly between my hands as I stood behind them, looking at their faces in the mirror, appraising them; I would run my finger down their cheeks as I described what I was about to do. All businesslike, I must repeat – nothing obviously sensual about it – and the men didn't know what it was, but when the haircut was over their whole bodies buzzed and they felt like a lobe of their brain had been hypnotized. Certain people have had that effect on me during my life – always somebody doing something meticulous, putting something in order. A teacher at school who made my brain tingle when she used a ruler to draw a line in my workbook; a stocktaker at the grocery store on every last Friday of the month, delicately piling tins of canned vegetables into neat rows.

I persuaded some of the men, the ones I felt could take it, to have their hair shampooed while they were at the shop, before the cutting, and I massaged their scalps as they lay with their necks slotted into the ceramic basin. I found the lumps and dips on their skulls and rubbed them – the parts that curved out or in, that revealed pleasure points. And the cutting itself – so rapid, so crisp, like brisk magic when I got it right. Word spread, men began to ask for me even when the barber was present, and then one day the barber came back from the Residence and said the President had asked for me. This was my proof that the President had eyes everywhere, that even the smallest shift in preference at the barber salon in the district didn't escape him. The barber was gracious in his defeat, but then he had no choice: the President had spoken.

The first time I cut the President's hair was in his own bathroom, a cavernous room with tiles stretching away as far as I could see. Two bodyguards escorted me through the Residence and then stood just outside the open bathroom door, ears pricked. There was a faint tremor in the President's hand when he greeted me. The bathroom lights did not flatter him – I hadn't realized he was so old. He was already smartly dressed for an evening function and he wanted his haircut to be so fresh the other men would be able to smell it, like cut grass on a warm evening. He sat on a plush armchair before the mirror, so low it made me lose my bearings briefly – I hadn't thought to bring one of the high chairs from the salon, and it meant that everything I did that evening was hunched. I bent over him to cover his shoulders with a cloth sheet and fastened the clasp at his neck, held his jaw between my hands, tilted his chin up and down and side to side. I sprayed his hair with faintly scented water and the drops spread finely across his strands. I cut briskly, with comb and scissors, and saw him lulled by the order and rhythm of the snipping, and used a razor along the nape of his neck and at the edge of his hairline. Then I whisked off the sheet, not letting a single cutting fall onto his suit. He was pleased, and the next time he let me shave and pluck him too. It was then that I began to convert my room above the salon into my glass box. At the end of my day's work at the City Residence, I longed for a sense of purity. I needed to purge myself of my guilt at not doing what I had come to the city to do. That's when I started sleeping with the window open, removing street clothes before I sat on the bed, and keeping the things around me – socks, glasses, belts – in rigid order; it was part of the purging.

She stirs. The sky is slowly preparing for dawn. She lifts her head, confused, and then stands quickly when she sees my face and pulls her dress back over her hips. Her long hair has fuzzed around her face and tangled its way down her back, and each strand seems to attract then absorb light so that it is luminous one moment, black the next. Around her mouth, wine is smudged like blood. As she leaves the veranda she knocks over the empty wine bottle, propelling it on a suicide roll off the side and onto the tiles below.

I follow her to the car and get into the passenger side obediently as she fights with the ignition until the motor splutters reluctantly into life, and we drive back along the dirt road, the stars already starting to fade, winding our way out of the valley. It is the coldest time of day, even in summer: the hour just before the sun reveals itself. I look at her bare legs, bumpy with cold. It used to fascinate me that my brother could casually hold his hand on her thigh beneath the table at supper with my mother and me. I would sneak peeks sideways at them – it was such a possessive gesture, but high enough on her thigh to be more than simply proprietary, and I would blush involuntarily each time I saw it, and they would laugh at me, not knowing the cause. To me, unschooled in intimacy, it seemed more daring – more charged – than if he had kissed her passionately in front of my mother.

'You know about me and the Commander, right?' she says, her eyes on the road ahead. 'I'm sure the chef told you. I'm his wife.'

Instinct makes me look at her ring finger, but there is no ring.

'Congratulations.' It comes out with bitterness, not what I'd intended.

She looks at me with her thick-lidded eyes showing concern, perhaps interpreting it as a younger brother's jealousy. 'He was in the same camp as we were. Your brother respected him deeply.'

Her long fingers on the steering wheel. Her smooth kneecap. The fat lobe of her ear. It is too much for me. 'Who kissed your wounds when they were fresh?' I ask. 'My brother? Or the Commander?'

Her pity dissolves visibly, she sets her mouth and jaw and we don't speak again until she tells me to get into the boot. This time I welcome the crawl into the cramped darkness.

13   *His portraitist*

Somebody must have fetched my old materials from my studio. The sight of these wrinkled metallic tubes, all half-squeezed, with their ends rolled tightly like slugs in distress, is not comforting. I think of the last time I touched them, the morning the President had changed colour and all the shades I'd mixed were wrong. My palette lies next to them, its surface thick from years of duty, and two canvasses are propped against the wall – I recognize them too, recognize the labour of stretching the canvas over the wooden frames and forcing staples into the spines to keep them tight.

This is the room where the President sat crumpled on the couch, photographs thrown at his feet. The furniture has been pushed aside, leaving long streak marks on the dusty floorboards – all but the couch, which is centre-stage, facing my easel. I fiddle with the bolts on the multi-jointed legs, sliding the sections together until the easel has shrunk to the right height. It is marked with accidental paint – this process always leaves a trail of evidence. My sketchbook is here too, a large and persistent reminder of all I have done wrong, and shards of charcoal lie in the groove at the bottom of the easel. Someone is familiar with my methods.

The Commander hovers at the door, uncertain for the first

time, perhaps cowed by the tools of skill, of expertise, that surround me. He lopes into the room and settles himself on the couch, crossing his legs and letting one slipper dangle from his foot.

I know that a portrait is one of the trappings of power, that each one I painted increased the President's control by a fraction; that the image of him, freshly rendered in oils, hanging in Parliament, had some value outside of itself, that it strengthened his legitimacy, and that it will do the same for this man sitting before me. The Commander's slipper drops from his foot, revealing long, thin toes. He puts his hand into the back pocket of his trousers and emerges with a fistful of purple blossoms, jacaranda.

'It's not just me you're painting,' he says, his fist still clenched around the petals. 'It's us.'

The President shows himself at the open door, flanked by guards. His head is held low; his jowls have lengthened and hang uneasily. He is wearing a purple dressing gown, tied with a knot at his thick waist. He shuffles towards the couch, and the Commander stands and throws the petals like confetti above his head. A few of them stick to his hair and shoulders, attaching themselves like barnacles to a rock, and he leaves them there, slumps onto the couch and then raises his head to look at me, his jaw steeled. The Commander sits jauntily beside him. For the first time I notice that his beauty is asymmetrical, that the halves of his face will have to be given separate attention. His profile seen from opposite sides would be different, like the two-faced gods of lore.

I flip open my sketchbook to a blank page, trying not to look at the previous sketches, and with a stick of charcoal I shape them on the page. I start with the President: his face is familiar, comforting; the lines are known and expected. I can be honest with him; it is what he always demanded. Within these lines I find new signals his body has sent for imprint on his skin – wrinkles and spots and patches of dryness. All these I document. What stirs in me, as my hand follows its own instincts, is what stirred for his wife in the observatory with the burning lamps when her zip caught on her underwear: pity.

14 *His chef*

I open the freezer and remove an ice-filled plastic bottle with a red lid. On the counter is a bowl of ice cubes in fridge water; next to it the chilled pastry dough is slowly making its way back to room temperature. My grandmother would call me a cheat if she could see what I'm doing, but I've found a way to avoid the excruciating layering process (dough, butter, dough, butter, dough) – this batch took me just an hour last night – although I haven't quite shaken the habit of rolling out the risen dough with an ice bottle or dipping my hands in the ice bowl whenever my fingertips become too warm. It's not really even necessary to do it this early in the morning. Working in huge restaurant kitchens as a cog in a wheel cured me of most of my sentimental attachments to certain processes, but this one never died.

Funny the things you see around here in the coldest hour of the night. The barber wasn't in his bed when I left the room and from the kitchen window I saw the Commander's wife crossing the courtyard barefoot, her sandals in her hand, her back hunched with the effort of trying to be quiet. Her hair looked like it had been tied up hastily, an attempt to hide its bushiness. Hair becomes bushy when someone puts their hands in it – the same used to happen to my wife. She depended on head massages before sex; her skull had erotic receptors that the rest of her body lacked. She would nudge her head up against my neck like a cat to remind me, then writhe and purr, and afterwards her cheeks would be bright pink and her hair nest-like from the added volume of the massage. I tried it on other women too, thinking it might be a secret weapon, but they became bored after a while and redirected my hands.

I'm surprised at my lack of jealousy. Perhaps, finally, I have accepted my age and have begun to look at the desire of young-er men indulgently, the way an old woman looks at a bride, not wanting to be back there again but still interested, still invested in the process and glad that other people have the energy to spend on it. She would have been my type, too, she would have made it difficult for me, would have extended the game, made me scour my imagination to find a way to entice her into my arms, just for a single night. That's what no woman other than my wife understood: it was never about the sex. She knew she had to make our daily interactions into a game that interested me. She would approach then retreat unpredictably, leave for days without explanation, purposefully ignore me at parties and speak only to other men. I thought she enjoyed it, but it took its toll in the end, and eventually she pleaded insanity as a way out. Or perhaps – I've not thought of it like this before – could it have been her most ambitious game of all, to make me constantly search for her sane mind: now I'm sane, now I'm not? To make me woo her each time her sane mind disap-peared and she had to be told who I was? She was very polite to me then, as polite as she always was to strangers – would try to make me feel at home in her wardroom, would invite me to help myself to tea or coffee, would ask me questions about my life and listen earnestly to my replies. Oh, I played along alright, it was fascinating to see if I could crack her open, get her to laugh and admit it had all been a game. She reminded me then of my daughter when she was very small, when she came with my wife to the airport to fetch me after I'd been away for a particularly long time. She obviously only faintly recognized me, and so she turned on all the charm her little mind could muster and sat in the back seat of the car next to me, entertaining me all the way home with stories about her friends and her pre-school and her pets.

My fingertips are getting too warm. I plunge them into the icy fingerbowl and then grip the solid bottle and keep rolling out the dough as evenly as possible, then use the rim of a glass to cut out even rounds and place them gingerly on an oiled baking tray. I seem to have lost my appetite. Normally I would pick at the ingredients as I go, using the excuse of quality control, so that by the time the meal is served I am already full, but since the seafood brunch I haven't eaten a morsel of the food I've prepared.

I have a feeling the Commander will be moving to the City Residence soon. He'll have to, to control the city and take up the full reins of power. The kitchens will be in disarray, probably looted and trashed, and it will be difficult re-establishing my supply lines. One thing I hope has been stolen is the linen, always over-starched so that it was heavy and sullen and scratchy to touch, and always made my eyes puff up and my fingers swell. That was in the days after I'd run away from home, when I was nothing but a busboy, clearing dirty plates and laying bright white tablecloths and making sure the cutlery was correctly spaced. Much later, when I'd been made sous-chef, I sent my mother some money for the bus fare to the city, but she didn't come. I am a self-made man, I used to say to myself whenever the guilt about abandoning her began to creep up on me. A self-taught chef. I used to wonder why they called it blind ambition because I know my eyes were wide open while I clawed my way up.

15 *His barber*

The red wine is taking its revenge today; since I woke my brain has felt tender and my body bruised, and there is a purple welt across my back from the slats of the deckchair. But stronger even than the dry pinch behind my eyes is this longing to be with her again, at any cost; right now I believe I would even disguise myself as him, wear his clothes, speak with his lilt, if it meant she would lie next to me once more and thread her fingers through my hair. She does not realize the power of her grace. It has always transfixed me. At least I have that to lay at her feet: fidelity.

The chef had a good look at me while I was in my bed this morning. He came back from the kitchens smelling of butter and yeast and stopped next to my bed for a long time. I pretended to be asleep, but I could sense his eyes searching for clues, and the wine stains on my lips probably gave me away, the woolliness of my hair, or the stench of last night's liquor hanging above my bed, or her scent just beneath it, the quiet smell of her hair and body. He took a deep breath and eventually shuffled away from the bed into the bathroom and stayed there for a long time.

The tools of my trade have just been miraculously delivered to the room by one of the guards – they must have broken into my shop to get them and terrorized my poor assistant to find out what I would need to groom the Commander. With this scene pounding in my head it is not an easy task to pick out a pair of scissors and a comb from the tangle that has been thrown into the bag, but it must be done – he is expecting me. The portraitist came back from his session yesterday sucked dry like an old lemon, with bits of paint all over his hands making them look diseased, and fell into bed without a word. He is a thin man who seems to have nourished himself mainly on his wife, and without her he is dissolving. Even the bony structures holding up his face have collapsed. When I crept back in early this morning, he shot up in his bed with his face towards me for a few chilling seconds, until I realized his eyes were closed and he was still asleep. He lay back down again very stiffly like somebody being lowered into a coffin, then he cried softly in his sleep and this morning he had a faint pattern of salt on his cheeks.

The guard thumps on the door to tell me to hurry up, so I grab my few utensils and wait for him to unlock the door. He walks beside me along the corridor around the courtyard. I look down at the square of grass and wish I could stand at the railing and look down on her again as she turns her face to the sun. The guard grunts and motions with his head to the stairwell and I realize that this is the first time I am going up and not down. The next floor is identical to ours, but with a guard outside every room – it is unnerving, but of course the desire begins to burn within me to know who is behind each door, what secrets are they guarding? And beneath that desire is a slight deflating – logic has told me that we are not the only prisoners, but to have the proof before me is still a small disappointment, a generalizing of our experience. Are they all being roomed in threes? Or are only the harmless ones put together and the real threats kept on their own to prevent plotting? Perhaps it's to my advantage that he thinks of me as harmless.

We cross to the other side of the floor and then climb another small staircase that curls around itself onto the top floor. There is only one entrance on this floor, a large wooden double door. The man standing outside unlocks it and lets us through into a room that I see immediately is the master bedroom, with a wall of glass through which there is a panoramic view of the entire valley, and even further – the City Residence is visible from here, a doll's house from this distance, and at night they must be able to see it lit up on its hill within the city.

'Quite a view,' says the Commander from an armchair against the wall. 'Our President certainly liked to keep an eye on things. His things, mostly.'

He stands, smiles languidly and wanders towards me with his hand outstretched. He is impeccably dressed, with a crisp line down the middle of each trouser leg and a collar as stiff and white as ice. I shake his hand because I have no choice, and he grips my elbow while we shake, an added intimacy. The guard opens a door behind us leading into the bathroom. One of these walls is also glass, revealing its own view of the valley, and the rest of the walls and the ceiling are covered with mirrors, even the floor, which gives the strange sensation of walking on water that has frozen over and could crack and give way at any step. The basin, toilet and bath do not obstruct the complete view of oneself in the mirrors as they are not built against the walls but in the centre of the room, little pods of gleaming steel. They too reflect: I can see my body truncated in the surface of the bath. The Commander is amused by my unsteady walk across the mirrors and laughs with the guard as I pick my way towards the basin.

'We need a chair,' I say quietly. 'A high one, preferably.'

The guard leaves and returns with the armchair the Commander had been sitting in. It is so low I will have to bend almost double to see what I am doing, but I position it beside the basin, facing the solid wall of mirror. 'Please…' I say to the Commander, and hold out my arm to the armchair like a butler ushering in a guest. He smiles and sits and crosses his legs and shakes out his gently curling hair, watching himself in the mirror. The guard hovers at the door, a few steps away from me, his eyes trained on me. I lay out the necessary items from my bag along the edge of the bath, in the order I will use them, then with a graceful arc I throw the soft plastic sheet over his front and clip it at the back of his neck so that no part of his clothing is exposed.

'I will be shampooing?' I say tentatively to the Commander.

He nods assent. I never ask a man if he would like a head massage with his shampoo, I simply do it. If you ask they feel embarrassed for saying yes – a man is not meant to chase sensual pleasure of that sort, they like to think a haircut is a brisk, businesslike transaction, something as necessary and as banal as flossing. I test the water with the inside of my wrist to make sure it won't burn him, roll a towel to place at the edge of the steel basin, and then gently rest the back of his neck on it, so that his head is lolling back slightly into the basin. I guide his head beneath the tap so that the water just catches his hairline and barely wets his skin. The hair strands darken and clot with the water; he will feel the slight weight of them pulling away from his head, uncreasing his forehead, and the warmth will spread like a tide across his skull to the back of his brain. I turn off the tap, leave his head in the basin, squeeze shampoo onto my palm and lather it. It will feel slightly cold against his warmed-up scalp, invigorating, and the hair will foam and become smooth against his skin.

I start with my fingertips at his hairline, working the gel into the roots along the edge of his forehead, and then just above his ears, his temples. Then I hold one hand against the top of his head and with the other in a soft fist I lather the underside of his skull, the lobe that protrudes just above the nape. I vary the pressure and motion and move slightly upwards over the lobe and to the flowering of the skull bone, where it makes its bulbous departure from the neck, and I stay here for a long time, rubbing with the flat of my palm against it, solid and circular. He keeps his eyes closed, but I notice his breathing becomes more pronounced and the artery at his neck reveals itself like the path left by a tunnelling creature. I check the water again against my wrist, then let it run warmly down from his hairline, watching the soap lose its clutch on his hair and leave the strands glossy and viscous. I lift another towel and place it in the basin beneath his head, then lift the edges and rub against his scalp quickly and with pressure, and tie it at his hairline so that he has a turban knotted at his forehead.

'You can lift your head now,' I say very quietly. He obeys.

The cutting itself is over in a few minutes, my scissors and hands flitting like butterflies about his hair, gently guiding his head in the direction I need it with two fingers on opposite sides of his jaw. The bits of wet hair drop heavily to his shoulders or slide down onto the sheet fanned about him on the armchair. He keeps his eyes closed, perhaps worried about the scissors so quick and close about his pupils. I unclasp the sheet and throw it off him before he has opened them, and he jumps slightly with the surprise, then looks down at his clothes for stray hairs. There are none; I have made sure of that. For a moment he looks sheepish, embarrassed to have felt such pleasure at the hands of another man, wondering if the guard noticed. They all look like that at the end. The trick is simply to ignore them at this point, motion with your head to the assistant at the till, remind them it is a cash transaction, no more, no less, and with relief they remember and sternly but quickly pay their bill and leave without a backward glance at you.

PART II

1 *His barber's brother's fiancée*

We are now installed in the City Residence, and as I try to fall asleep on our first night here already the guilt is crouching at the back of my mind. What struck me while I was carrying my suitcase up the staircase earlier today is that after the shock of a forced changing of the guard, the follow-up processes are in themselves rather insignificant. Human beings dispose of each other, set themselves up in the place of the deposed, and then go about their daily tasks: you shave at the ex-President's basin, examine yourself in his mirror, pack your old socks in his underwear drawer. That in turn made me think about contamination, and whether a bad person leaves behind bad things in his space, excretes badness like foul air: can you catch it like a cold? I watched my husband – the Commander, he calls himself now – sitting on the edge of the bathtub, waiting for the bath to fill, and as he submerged his body in the water, I thought of the President lying in that same tub and his pores against the same marble. When he climbed into bed next to me, his skin still warm and fragrant from the bathwater, I didn't want him to touch me.

He wanted to carry me across the threshold of the President's bedroom in his arms when we arrived, but I told him it was a sick joke and, unnerved, started unpacking my clothes into the cavernous wardrobes. The bedroom has a view out over the city from the balcony: you can see as far as the sea and the stunted palms dotting the concrete parking lots from the one side, and from the other the mountains are visible. The air is oppressive, as it always is in the city at this time of year. You forget the heat when you're up in the mountains the way you forget what pain feels like as soon as it's over; memory sieves out pain, dulls it with time, an essential trick to condemn us to repetition. As we wound our way down from the Summer Residence, I could see the pollution bowling through the city, a hot soup of toxins, and my ears popped, taking me by surprise – I hadn't realized how high up we'd been. It felt, in truth, like a descent into hell, but I couldn't tell my husband that. He was excited, this was what he'd been waiting for: reclaiming space, in the name of freedom. The city had been secured with very little violence and we'd been told that the people simply wanted to get on with their lives.

I can't sleep. He has lost himself in his dreams, and mumbles each time he turns over. I walk out to the balcony to watch the heat rising from the city, from the pavements and the tops of buildings and swimming pools, making the lights flicker more violently. The Residence is perched at the top of the highest ground in the city, lording it over the rest of the Presidential District. The guards, from habit I suppose, have closed off all the roads around it for the night, forcing late-night commuters to give it a wide berth. The District is quiet, relieved that the sun has abandoned its siege. There are signs of struggle – the blackened lobby of a hotel, sandbags layered where glass once was, a stairway that leads to nothing, roads with pieces of concrete levered from them by explosions, looking like hunks of black ice floating in a frozen river in late winter – but mostly the city hums on oblivious to the changes. I can't decide if that is right or wrong, but I'm disappointed regardless; I had imagined, I suppose, that we would be welcomed like homecoming heroes, feted and applauded, and have roses flung at our vehicle. But still nobody will believe what the President did, and even if they do, the rumours will soon fly that we will do no better.

I miss the barber; I took for granted the pleasure that came from knowing that we were under the same roof, hearing the same night sounds, feeling the same cool wind from the valley. He's no longer at the Summer Residence; of the three men in his room, only the portraitist has remained there, and that was by choice, because he was told his wife wouldn't be released yet. I imagine the barber has either tried to make for our home village on the coast, or he is still on his way to the city – without the benefit of a motorcade it will take him much longer than it did me. My husband will employ him when he gets here – he said the trial haircut he gave him was magical, which struck me as a strange word to use. And of course he insisted that the chef come with us – he trusts him completely – and already he has the kitchens in working order again. He doesn't serve us personally anymore, or at least he didn't last night at dinner, and I even miss feeling *his* gaze – reverential, appreciative – on me between courses. It amused my husband, this wrinkled chef's infatuation with me, and made me feel desired, desirable. He must have been attractive once, before his skin went stale and his belly ballooned, as tends to happen to men in old age. He often looked at my arm, trying to catch a glimpse of the scars on the inside of it, the ones he touched over the steaming pot and feels in some way that he owns. I am not proud of them,

I would not go so far as to casually roll my arm over while he was presenting the dessert and let him see them, they are not a badge of honour nor a tool of titillation. The barber is the only one who knows what to do with them: show neither pity nor horror, let them neither increase nor deflect desire, but simply acknowledge their presence. I had to guide him the first time, on the balcony in the vineyards, but each time after that, when I managed to free him from his room and hide in a knot with him somewhere secret, he understood how to touch them. The chef must have noticed what was happening – he saw me that morning crossing the courtyard, but he has said nothing.

My husband has proven fickle when it comes to the prisoners: the ones he feels have in some way proved their usefulness he has released, while others who are more closely implicated have remained in the Summer Residence. He likes having them there, the way a cat likes having a lizard to play with, with no intention of killing it, but perhaps severing its tail, safe in the knowledge that it can grow another. The photographs have been distributed throughout the city, blown up into macabre billboard posters, a decision I didn't agree with. My husband says that now nobody has an excuse not to know.

I can smell the sea on the wind. The promenade is usually wet with waves at high tide, the miles of concrete failing at their task to keep out the sea. The sea air is laced with something else too, the sweet smokiness of night-time cooking fires that reminds me of the rubbish tips back home which festered daily in the sun and bred over-sized wild flowers that opened in the evenings, masking the stink with their fragrance. It was a playground to me, each discarded object a wealth of future possibilities. After my parents died and I lived alone in the cottage, I decorated it entirely with things I'd found at the tips and restored to a state of usefulness and beauty: I sanded down wood, defogged glass, turned a stack of old iron wheels into a table, painted crates for chairs, used a car door as a desk. There were other people at the tips, usually making fires and digging around for food, which made it less desolate, but there was always an imminent danger that threw into relief my pleasure at getting home safely with my hoard. It was a solitary activity. My fiancé at the time – the barber's brother – wanted to come with me; he said there were gangs at the tips who preyed on solitary females, but I refused. It was a necessary danger, vital to me: I couldn't believe the joy that came from salvaging discarded things and making them my own.

Once I found an old wooden wardrobe lying on its side, in ankle-deep rubbish, and managed to get it upright to force open the door. Inside was a thick grey coat, ideal for winter. I took it home and let it soak in soap in the bath for a few hours, but when I began to scrub the coat by hand, I could feel that something had been sewn into the silk lining, that something was wadded in there and rustling. I lifted the coat out of the water, unpicked the lining and gingerly peeled it back. Inside I found damp banknotes – hundreds of them – and a document from an earlier regime, something that looked like an identity card for a police force. The name on the document was illegible; it had bled from the bathwater. I lived off the banknotes for a year after that – like a queen, in fact, allowing myself all kinds of extravagant foods and luxury goods imported from overseas. I didn't tell anybody about it, not even my fiancé – he would have told me to save the money, or to find the owner of the coat and somehow return it. I had to hide all evidence of my affluence (rare cheeses, good wine, aged meat) before he arrived for our pre-lunchtime trysts. He would come straight from the boat, reeking of fish, scrub his hands at the sink with scented soap, and then we'd sleep together as quickly as we could before he had to return home to his mother and younger brother for lunch. Only once he spotted an empty wine bottle outside my back door and looked suspiciously at the silver-inscribed label like it was a mortal enemy. All those secret, stolen pleasures – the rubbish tips, the treasure hoarding, the illicit sex – was it all to reclaim what was stolen from me? The right to two parents who would watch me ease my way into adulthood, who could mend my moral compass when I broke it, who could give me armfuls of love so that I wouldn't have to search always for a man's embrace? On the terrace, the city lights blur despite my refusal to cry or to let remorse get the better of me. I turn back into the darkened bedroom and crawl between the sheets, inching closer to my husband, nesting against his warm body.

2 *His chef's daughter*

She hasn't shifted her position for four hours. I keep note of these things because I have to. I've been sitting in the low arm-chair, reading, and she's been sitting in the hard-backed chair she likes, with her hands in her lap, looking at the clock on the wall. I think she likes the symmetry of it. If I look at her for too long my face starts to burn, the heat a harbinger of such sadness that I have no choice but to ignore it. Watching a parent like this, watching her stare at a wall for four hours, forget she has a daughter, lose all interest in my life, is not something I would wish even on my father. I don't know how to deal with this excess of emotion so I shelve it, knowing it will come out later, when I drink myself to the point of being vulnerable.

It has been a month now since the coup. I was with my lover when it happened, lying drowsily next to him, grateful for his presence as I slipped out of sleep. We heard distant, constant gunshots and then people streaming out of buildings into the street. He got up and pulled aside the curtain and said they were all gazing up at the Presidential Residence, chatting as if it were a street picnic. It was festive, come to think of it – I lay in the bed feeling excited, as if it were a snowy day and I didn't have to go to classes, or the electricity grid had crashed for the whole city and nobody could go to work. I think we all secretly like those kinds of mini-catastrophes that let us off the hook for a few hours or days, that let us guiltlessly shirk routine. I didn't worry about my father's safety when we heard gunfire, though I knew he was in the Residence kitchens, and I'm still not worried, even though we haven't heard from him since then. I've been observing him since I was old enough to walk and I know he'll do whatever it takes to survive.

Unfortunately people always say I look like him. When I was a little girl, and too young to know any better, I took it as a compliment, but later on I noticed how people looked embarrassed after they'd said it, when they realized I might be offended at having a man's features. I've spent far too much time in front of mirrors, wishing parts of myself away – I remember mirrors I've used in my life the way other people remember men they've slept with, that's how intimate I've been with them. I can recall precisely which ones distorted the size of my nose, which ones showed skin blemishes during the day with the sunlight streaming into my room but not at night by lamplight, which ones made my legs look longer, which ones unfailingly depressed me, which ones gave me hope. So many half-truths. If I could somehow get a composite image of all these reflections, maybe I would know the whole truth about my own face and body. The mirror in my mother's en-suite bathroom is of the depressing variety, by day or by night, no matter which angle. I even tried standing on the edge of the bathtub to get a different view of my legs in the reflection, but the verdict was no better than when I balanced on the toilet seat. Ironic, considering this is meant to be a place where you go to feel better about yourself, or, in her case, to remember who you are and why you went crazy. When she takes a look at herself in that mirror she probably won't want to remember, but she's older and must have negotiated a truce with her body long ago, laid down the hatchet, raised the white flag, whatever she had to do to achieve an uneasy peace. I look forward to that time in my life, when I can blame the stretchmarks on a baby and not on my own inconsistencies, although I do remember asking my mother once how old she expected her face to look every time she glanced at the mirror, and she said eighteen. I asked a lot of people the question after that, and they all said eighteen. My mother said she sometimes got a shock if she went to the bathroom in the middle of the night and caught a glimpse of her face; she said it was like finding an intruder in your house, so she stopped turning on the bathroom light and that's when she had her bad fall. Split her head open. That's unrelated to the madness, which was the result of a different kind of splitting: a marriage falling apart.

After my initial excitement about the coup, I realized I had to come here to her, to protect her if there was any trouble. My lover and I dressed quickly and I packed a bag of clothes and some tins of food, and he walked me to the home through the crowded streets. Word had spread fast. One of the bars was handing out free beer and shots with a hastily sprayed, multicoloured sign hung over the entrance: 'Brace yourself for the revolution!' The owner of a cake shop had set up a trestle table in the street and was handing out cream pies for people to throw at an effigy of the President. Things got stranger and more serious in the days that followed; my lover fled the city – he said he had no choice, given who his father is – and I moved into my mother's room permanently. I still feel that I can't leave her in the home alone with things so uncertain. I prefer to call this place a home; it makes it sound as if she's simply been put in an old people's home before her time and not in an institution. It's not really an institution, just a care facility, an expensive one, but there's no denying the fact that she's mad. Yesterday I occupied myself for over an hour thinking about all the different ways you can say that she is crazy: off her cracker; in the loony bin; lost the plot; lost her marbles; loopy; gone bananas; lost her mind; bonkers; stark, raving mad. I guess that means it must have happened to a lot of people. My father paid the bill, blood money, with his fat salary from the President. The management hasn't yet received payments for any of their guests this month, with all the changes, so we're OK for now, but I hope he starts paying up again soon otherwise they're going to kick her out.

I went out this morning to get milk and tea bags and found people grouping around posters that had been glued to walls like theatre bills, horrific images that are blown-up photographs of mangled people. The new government has already begun its propaganda push, it seems. I didn't hang around or try to edge my way to the front of the crowd; there is a delicate line between knowing too little (ignorance) and knowing too much (perversity), and around me in the little group people were panting, whether from horror or excitement I couldn't tell. My father probably knew it was going on – he was close enough to the President in a non-political capacity for the President to confide in him the way one confides in one's plants while watering them on a sunny balcony. He's not the grovelling type, though, my father, that's why men in power like him – they recognize themselves in him, utterly committed to one man alone: himself. On my way back to my mother, I stopped at the university campus with its stuccoed buildings built in imitation of something grander, and it reminded me of the President's Summer Residence. The campus was deserted except for a few homeless people who had broken into one of the classrooms to take shelter from the fighting and were trying to build a fire with broken-down bookshelves. I was secretly hoping that university life would continue unaffected, that the bell jar of academia would have protected my routine there. I had grown stronger in my first semesters there – I could feel it as palpably as weight gain – and was beginning to contemplate embarking on the search for the end of the string that could lead me to untangle the knot that is my life as my father's daughter, as my lover's woman, as my sick and absent mother's child. Now I feel I have lost sight of where that end is and will never find it again.

I spent time at the President's Summer Residence years ago, when my father was still obliged to cook for him on holiday. It is perched above the vineyards in the valley, a child's dream with its courtyards and passages and sculpture garden. My mother and I were terrified to meet him, utterly intimidated. The first day he and his wife invited my father and mother to lunch with them, a generous gesture it seemed, but my mother suspected it was designed to boost the President's wife's ego more than her own. She said to me, 'She is going to rub my face in my inferiority the way you rub a puppy's nose in its own shit,' and she didn't want to get dressed for the lunch because she didn't know what she was going to say. We sat in her bedroom, like two naughty children, and she locked the door so my father couldn't come in and drag her out, but as soon as he had abandoned her she began to feel guilty and put on the red dress she knew he liked and painted her lips and ventured out to the dining room. I heard the murmuring and scraping of cutlery on crockery stop in its tracks for a few seconds, presumably when she appeared at the doorway, and then continue as before, at a slightly higher volume because of the effort of pretending nothing had happened.

My mother and I would go for long walks down the winding road to the valley base, and wander between the rows of grapevines. I tasted wine for the first time there, at one of the vineyards, which was almost as momentous an occasion as my first kiss – my stomach burned and my head grew hot and my mother laughed at me all the way home because I had the hiccups.

My father never let me sit in the Summer Residence kitchen to observe him while he was working, but I spied on him several times, to try to understand what kind of magic he was doing in there with all those strange utensils and live creatures; usually he caught me and I would get a hiding and run to my mother, who would look at my father like he was a monster, and that would make my attempt worthwhile. The President and his wife were hopeless with me. I was a precocious little child, already full of big ideas and deep thoughts, but they would converse with me as if I were an imbecile. Once I bumped into the President in the sculpture garden; he had been watching me, silently, and I had been so immersed in pretending the sculptures were alive that I'd backed into him and screamed when he moved, thinking one of the statues had come to life. He looked at me strangely, bent down to my eye level, and said with a pause between each word, 'Do… you… like… ice… cream?' I ran away, more because I was offended by his question than from fear. His wife insisted on giving me a hug each time she saw me, and she would press me into her bosom and leave make-up on my clothes. When I grew older, I regaled the other children in my class with these stories of my intimacy with the President, and they gazed at me impressed. It created a definite aura – something so effective it was almost visible, like a halo – and I milked it for all it was worth; it was the most effective weapon in my arsenal in the war with other girls to attract boys.

I'm skirting the issue, but there were other children there too. The President's kids, two of them: a girl who was years younger than me and a boy who was years older. Five years older. Come to think of it, the best evidence anybody could present of the President's capacity for cruelty is his son, who must have learned it from someone. I know he'll be somewhere safe – like my father, he is doggedly committed to self-preservation – but that doesn't stop the need I feel for him burrowing its way into my gut like a parasite.

My mother stirs, finally, and asks me for some water, very politely, like I'm a stranger. It's time for me to start drinking too.

3   *His portraitist's wife*

I can't deny I'm a magpie; I've always loved shiny things. Even when I was little my mother said I used to pick up anything in the street that gleamed and she would have to wrench my hand open to throw it away. I could spot a dropped coin from metres away. My favourite was the glimmering grains in the pavement concrete – I don't know what they were, bits of glass that got mixed in with the concrete perhaps; at night the streetlights would make them dance as I walked and to my mother's horror I would squat on the pavement and scratch at them, believing I could take them home. My grandmother had a wooden box full of jewelled buttons that I would spend hours polishing with a handkerchief and laying out in long, magical rows. So it was only natural that I moved on to bigger, better shiny things as I got older. Real jewels and rare metals, and crystal too. All my lovers knew they had to keep the magpie in me satisfied. And then I met my husband and renounced publicly all things glittering. But my father secretly kept me well stocked with my heart's desires, and I still maintain it was worth it for the look on my mother's face when she first met my husband at one of his exhibitions. The masterpiece was the shattered fragments of a raw egg that he had dropped from the tenth floor of a building onto the pavement below. My family was his only audience.

I don't think about him much, even though I know he's under the same roof. He made a fool of himself last week, calling down to me while I was exercising in the sculpture garden. He wants me to share this baby with him; ever since I fell pregnant he has been niggling away at me to include him, but it is none of his business, that's how I feel. He had all kinds of tricks to try to feel a part of it: stocking the fridge with champagne, buying lemons, making hundreds of useless sketches to present me with when I've popped it out. After I told him I was pregnant, he observed me even more closely than before. I'd grown used to his constant scrutiny – not critical, but worshipping: smelling clothes I'd left behind on chairs, getting a jolt to his heart if he recognized my silhouette in the car in front of him, gazing at me from the bed with love in his eyes even when I was doing something ablutionary, like plucking my eyebrows. But he really turned it up a notch after the baby was announced and it threw me; I would turn around in the bath to find him staring at me silently, or wake in the middle of the night to see him watching my belly rise and fall in the dark. Before the baby, early in our marriage, I felt it was the kind of attention I deserved, that he was the only man who grasped my true worth, and I thrived under his gaze. I would even let him draw me naked. But there was something infantile about his obsession that made it quickly become tiresome.

There is a calm that comes from thinking only about oneself; I would venture so far as to say it is the only true freedom. I discovered that early on, encouraged by my mother's good example. Self-devotion – and by that I mean devotion to oneself – takes time to perfect, like all skills worth developing, and requires extreme discipline. I am grateful for the time I invested in the process now – in this situation it stands me in very good stead. I am not in the least bit concerned about my father or mother and their fate after the coup; they're either lying murdered in their country house or they've flown their private jet out of the country and resettled in one of their meticulously decorated overseas houses. My mother was the type to fill a house with invaluable artwork and priceless furniture even when she had a small child (me) and then to lock me in my room as punishment if I destroyed anything accidentally during a slumber party. She never cooked a single meal – we had cooks, but she hardly used them; we would meet at a restaurant for most meals. She has an unfortunate stutter – it's rumoured as a result of a childhood trauma, but she's never told me about it – so despite her excellent breeding the only man who would marry her was my father, who was compensating for his disfigured face (an accident with hot oil when he was a child) by pursuing power as if it promised him deliverance, and perhaps it has, if they've murdered him.

The President's wife is in a room down the corridor; she is allowed to visit me every few days and bores me witless. It is unfortunate that we share the same name because she thinks it gives her the right to expect intimacy with me; she's always trying to tell me secrets, whispering them conspiratorially even though nobody is listening, and then looking at me greedily when she's done, expecting me to tell her mine. She dissolves into tears every time she mentions her husband, frets about her children even though they are safely ensconced overseas, asks me repeatedly if I think she's looking old and then disappears into my bathroom to look at herself in the mirror. She pulls at various lobes and rolls and dangling bits so that her face smooths out and then when she lets go her skin creases like a discarded glove. I asked if she'd been allowed to see her husband and she said that she had, and then pulled her face into its coarse, secretive look and asked if I'd been allowed to see mine.

'I chose not to,' I said, just to shock her, and it worked.

She put her hand to her breast, said, 'Has something happened?' and then stared pointedly at my stomach.

I didn't expect to feel this way about the child. I hated how pregnant women at garden parties would bond over the minutiae of their bodily functions as if they were a different species from the rest of us, and I imagined it would make me feel invaded, the baby like a tapeworm curled in my stomach, feeding off me. Instead, it felt like I was feeding off it, that it was my own private regenerator: my hair thickened, my skin glowed, my fingernails grew more robust; it even changed the way I slept so that my dreams were full of beautiful, restless detail. As soon as my stomach showed, women looked at me with quick envy and men couldn't take their eyes off me. It is a strange, public trial, being heavily pregnant, being forced to walk around with proof of your sex act before you, visible to the world. Most of the time you can only guess what – if anything – other people are getting up to, but in those few months of exposure you know everybody knows what you did, and for a different kind of woman, not used to that kind of scrutiny, it must be excruciating. I suppose your skin betrays you too, in the end – it gives you away, despite your best efforts – but it discloses the dirty truth of what is about to happen to you (death) whereas pregnancy tells the seamy truth of what you did a few months before.

I think the problem will come when it is old enough to speak. My mother believed I was born evil and had to be made good through severe discipline and by not paying me any attention so that I wouldn't think I was entitled to anything, not even her love. She would drag me along with her to tea parties or committee meetings and leave me outside to play on my own in the garden, like a domesticated animal, where I would scratch around to find wild fennel to suck on like a sweet, or I would dig up bulbs and try to eat them like apples. My father says she was wonderful with me when I was a newborn – she loved that stage and craved it afterwards – but he refused to have another. She loved my wordless snuffling and simple needs, but it scared her when I grew old enough to talk, not because I could talk back, but because I might decide independently that I didn't like her; so she acted first and decided she wouldn't like me, and saved herself a lot of hurt. My father marvelled at me, and still does; not at the kind of person I am or at the things I've done, but at my intact, unmarked face – I think he didn't fully believe that his deformity could never be passed down to me, and he would often call me over to his side when I was small, hold my face up to the light and turn it from side to side.

He gave me an early appreciation for aesthetics. My work later on, as a food beautician, was more about appearances, which is a perversion of aesthetics: making something seem what it is not. I fell into it – nobody decides to be a food beautician – but immediately liked the duplicity that is its basis: soap foam had to be scooped on top of beer, vegetables had to be lacquered, raw meat had to be sprayed brown (when cooked, it looks too dry and shrivelled for a close-up), plastic had to be melted to form cheese strands with just the right consistency. It was a world I could control and manipulate, that required meticulous attention to detail and an eye for deception. My husband took it far too seriously, told me that I was an artist like him, that the only difference between us was that the President wanted the truth and my boss wanted anything but. I didn't need to work – despite the fallout over my marriage, even my mother wouldn't have dared to question this right to leisure – but it amused me, got me out of the apartment and let me spend time on trivial details that comforted me with their smallness.

I think I did once love my husband, right at the beginning. I say this as if I'm an old woman looking back on the vastness of my married life, but I feel that old sometimes, and I know what it's going to be like before it even hits me. It might just be the lumpiness of pregnancy, the dragging, the slowing down, or the fact that you age twice as quickly once you're married. After the initial bloom of it, the thrill of using those new words, 'my husband', it began to feel like I had hit a dead-end, ploughed straight into a solid wall, a dread sense of the complete shutting down of all possibility. From the earliest years of girlhood, it had been the dominant mystery in my life – whom would I marry? And when? – and suddenly it was solved, overnight, and the unseen force that had propelled me onwards all those years wilted. I think that's why people stop caring when they get old: there are no more mysteries to solve; you know what job you've chosen, whether you've had children, how many, girls or boys, what their names are, what childbirth felt like, where you're living, how much money you earn, who your husband is, what he does, how often he makes love to you, whether your face wrinkled at the eyes or the mouth first. And then you get old enough to start putting pressure on younger people to solve their mysteries, because deep down you want them to suffer the same slow creep of boredom that you did.

The Residence is quiet now. Most people seem to have left, or been moved. There is no sign of human presence around me except for the guard who sometimes coughs outside my door on his rounds. It is just me and this child within me who must know that it is almost time for it to emerge into this sick, sad world and fight to have its way.

4 *His barber's brother's fiancée*

This morning my husband had already left the Residence by the time I woke up. Sleep lay heavily on me, an almost physical force pinning me to the bed, and I had to throw it off like an attacker and drag myself to the bathroom, feeling wounded, but briefly grateful that my husband never leaves the toilet seat up, as I'm entirely capable of sitting down without looking and feeling the hard, cold porcelain bowl hit against my bones instead of the flat safety of the seat. The day's beauty revealed itself through the bathroom windows, an oppressive beauty, demanding some kind of worship of me, and left me feeling, once again, vaguely guilty. I dressed and went down to breakfast to find the Residence bustling with servants and party officials, all of whom greeted me ceremoniously. I know it will be all too easy to become soft here, to start to expect things: in the dining room, breakfast was laid out for me, a myriad of choices. As I ate, the swinging doors into the kitchens opened to reveal the chef, whom I was glad to see and invited to sit with me. He told me the kitchens were almost destroyed from looting, but slowly he was piecing things together again. He was perky and solid; the move to the city had blown new air into him like a blow-up toy. He stole a glance at my arm as I ate grapefruit.

I've spent the day walking through the Presidential District, watching people, seeing how shop owners have improvised with broken windows or missing doors so that they can keep trading despite the wreckage, and the mood is upbeat; groups have gathered under the few intact trees to share stories and borrow tools. I look at my reflection in a large, unbroken shop window, pretending to look at the wares behind it. My slimness always takes me by surprise; I suppose because of my height I don't think of myself as small, but it is pleasing to see my narrowness: my body promises ascetic pleasure, not full-bodied. Somebody from within the shop stirs, thinking I'm interested in buying, and I change my focus and look beyond my reflection and into the shop.

A young man, a boy really, emerges at the door to my left and says, 'I've never done a cut for a woman before... but I'd be happy to try.'

I look at the storefront: 'BARBER' it says, in thick gold letters. I look at the boy again, and he looks back at me open-faced – I don't think he meant to offend me. I know this must be the barber's shop, my barber's shop. He said it was close to the Residence and that his assistant would probably still be hanging around it, unsure what else to do. I lift my hand, release my hair from its clasp, and follow him into the shop.

It is dark inside, and one can observe passers-by unnoticed – he must have seen me looking at myself. There are no wares in the windows other than a few sideways-sprouting potted plants, and the shop is tidy but bare. I can see that things have been pulled off the walls and not yet replaced and many of the bulbs embedded around the mirrors have burst their filaments or been smashed; others flicker in and out of consciousness –

my reflection jumps out then recedes. The assistant wheels a high red chair to me and motions for me to sit down. He has a spray bottle filled with liquid and from a jar of milky water he lifts a pair of scissors with long blades and a thin-toothed comb.

'I would wash your hair first normally,' he says, nervously screwing the spray tip back onto the base, 'but the basin's cracked.'

I look over my shoulder at it and see that the crack has branched out like a lightning rod, splitting the basin into small shards that are still clinging to each other. He whips a plastic sheet over my front and ties it too tightly at my neck. The first squirt misfires and he hits me in the eye with the spray and then agitatedly wipes around my eye with a small towel, as if he's hoping I won't notice. A fine mist forms around my head as he works, and I feel my hair pull gently on my scalp. Each time the fickle light bulbs illuminate, the mist becomes gold. He begins to pull at the strands with the comb, but my hair knots around it and he curses under his breath.

'I'm not used to hair this long,' he says, embarrassed. 'Men's hair never knots.'

I smile at him in the mirror, then wince as he pulls at the comb. 'Is this your salon?' I ask, between tugs.

His eyes flicker at my reflection, as if he's trying to see if he can trust me. 'No,' he says eventually. 'The owner went missing during the… um…' He trails off, unsure what to call it.

'The coup?' I offer.

He nods silently, frowning with concentration.

'What's he like, the owner?' I ask as he attacks another knot.

'He always treated me well,' he responds. 'I started off just sweeping and cleaning, ordering stock, that kind of thing, but then he taught me some things and let me work with customers when he wasn't here, when he was up at the Res…'

He stops abruptly, catching himself, and glances at my reflection again, to see if I'm listening.

'Was he good at what he did?' I ask, ignoring his slip-up.

He has managed to get my wet hair into long, separate, knot-free strands and is now brandishing the scissors. His face lights up.

'Men came from all over the city to him. He didn't turn anybody away. Sometimes there would be a queue out onto the pavement.' He points to my hair. 'How much?'

I shrug. 'Just a trim. Straighten it out.'

He begins to snip, not in layers, but straight across the edge of my hair, using the comb occasionally to measure the next cut against the one he just made. I let him work in silence. In the mirror I see a man pause outside the shop, peer through the window and then rummage through his pockets. Not finding anything, he keeps walking.

It still makes me uncomfortable to have my hair cut by someone other than my mother; to have a stranger perform a task that is so intimate – cutting the very fibres that grow from your head – is somewhat vulgar to me, distasteful. I always wonder how people long ago could let their servants bathe them, scrub their backs and pour clean, hot water over their naked bodies to rinse afterwards. Once a hairdresser pointed out that I had a patch of dry scalp near my hairline, and I was so indignant that I never went back to her – she had broken the unspoken contract never to make a judgement of me when I was at my most vulnerable, letting a stranger look at my scalp. My mother's haircuts were unpredictable (I never knew what my hair would look like afterwards), but they were safe because she wasn't a stranger. After she died I tried to teach myself to cut my own hair but it made me too sad and I would end up staring at myself in the mirror and crying. Not for long, because crying is not designed for doing alone, and tears soon dry up unless there is a witness to them.

They were simple people: my father was a fisherman like all the men in the village and my mother was a fisherwoman, unlike all the women in the village. She'd been doing it for years before they got married, but she wasn't militant about it; she didn't demand to be allowed to fish, she was simply too good at it for them to refuse her, and meek enough that they couldn't feel threatened. She and my father always worked on separate crews after I was born, just in case, but that one day his crew was desperate for another member and she took a chance and went out with them. They drowned together; the survivors said that they were last seen clinging to each other in the water. It probably made them sink faster, the double weight. I expected that losing them would make me stronger, that I would grow hard and self-reliant with time, the way wood eventually becomes stone-like with age, but instead it created a need in me for a man, just one, who would make me his first priority; friends weren't good enough – they had obligations to too many people. A lover alone could ward off the loneliness enough to let me function, to venture out into the world.

My fiancé, the barber's brother, was my first lover. The most difficult time of the day for me after my parents drowned was the early afternoon, those no-man's-land hours after lunch, when the light is too stark for shadows, and drowsiness made me desperate. I worked from home then, making baskets and decorated bags for the market, and he would come back to my flat after he'd eaten at home, telling his mother he had to return to the docks. I depended on him coming; it was always such a relief when I heard him let himself in at the door and come straight to me as I lay on the bed. We wouldn't undress, it was not the time for it and we'd already let desire run its course during his morning visit. We simply lay there and I would beg him not to let me fall asleep because my grief fed off afternoon sleep and I would wake up disoriented and listless. He was a bulwark against my sadness. Later on, at dusk, when he had gone, I would see the indent his head had left on the pillow next to me, a small reminder of his presence, that he had been there, that somebody in the world knew about me and my life and its detail. As I've grown older the time of day that I find most depressing has changed; now it is the mornings, but I suppose that is not unusual – for most people waking up reminds them of things they'd rather forget.

'How do you like it?' asks the assistant, standing back from me to look at his handiwork.

He picks up a mirror and holds it behind me with a flourish, so I can see the back of my head in the wall-mirror. There's nothing much to see, other than my hair ends in a rigidly straight line and already starting to frizz slightly as they dry. Something else catches my eye in the mirror, a man whose shape has become familiar, pausing outside the shop, looking at it critically, tracing a faint crack in the glass with his finger.

'Don't you like it?' the assistant says, worried.

'No, it's fine, of course I like it,' I say, trying to smile, stealing another look at the reflection of the man outside. The assistant follows my eyes and then turns to look at the man himself. He drops the scissors, rushes outside and throws his arms around the man's neck, almost lifting him off the ground. He really must have believed the barber was dead. The barber smiles down at him, listens patiently as words begin to pour out of the assistant's mouth in relief. The assistant follows him into the shop, then remembers me and falls silent. In the time it takes the barber's eyes to adjust to the darkness of the shop, I manage to untie the plastic sheet around my neck, pull it aside and step down from the high chair. My damp hair clings to the back of my shirt.

'Leave us, will you?' he says, and for a horrible second I think he's talking to me until the assistant slowly takes his wallet from the counter and lopes out of the room, stealing a backwards glance at us. The barber moves towards me, lifts me under my arms and places me back onto the high chair. He swivels the chair so that I'm looking at my reflection again in the mirror. A bulb fizzes, then blows. He stands behind me and looks for a long time at me, using the mirror as our medium, perhaps afraid of what will happen if we look directly at each other, using his reflection as a decoy so he can see if I'm going to shoot at it mistakenly or lay down my arms. There is an accusation in his eyes – one that has lingered since our first night together, that I cannot dispel no matter what I say to him. He scans my face for any sign that I am searching for someone else, perhaps blurring my eyes so that the shape of his jaw changes slightly, or that his hair curls a little less. He has shaved off his beard and he rubs the fresh stubble with his hand, as if inviting me to protest, to ask him to grow another, so that the resemblance to his brother is maintained. I notice a small mole above his lip and a faint scar at the base of his chin and will myself to remember them: they are his own private markings, they are what his body alone saw fit to do to his skin. I reach up my hand without turning to look at him, using the mirror to locate the scar, and trace it with my fingertip. I have passed his test: he swivels me around to face him, kissing me as he lifts me from the chair, and I curl my legs around his hips. He carries me to the door to the backroom, nudges it open with his shoulder, and closes it again with his foot, where the darkness is complete.

Before I leave, he says he wants to show me something, and fumbles on the wall in the dark for the light switch. A bare fluorescent bulb dangles from the ceiling, starkly outlining rows and rows of shelves, extending from wall to wall like stacks in a library. At first I don't see what's on them, absorbed in smoothing out my skirt to rid it of creases. I look up to see him holding out a small glass jar to me, filled with something fibrous and dark, and around me on the shelves are hundreds of glass jars, all containing different shades of the same matter.

'These are yours,' he says. 'I collected them from my brother's pillow the mornings after I knew you'd climbed through the window and slept there.'

The jar is full of hairs, thick ones that I recognize immediately as my own. I take down another jar from the shelf and find it is filled with stubble and short hair, probably a week's worth of clippings from the shop floor, swept up and bottled.

'Good thing nobody got in here,' he says, surveying the shelves. 'Can you imagine what it would look like if they had?'

5 *His chef's daughter*

My mother always spoke about making love in rapturous terms. She was first obliged to tell me what it was when I was five and went to find her when I heard the telephone ringing late at night. My father thought I was an intruder and jumped up naked from the couch in attack mode, and my mother quickly put on her dressing gown and steered me back to bed, promising they would explain everything in the morning and hoping I would forget all about it. At first light I arrived on their bed, woke them, and demanded an explanation. After they'd told me that they were 'revealing their true love to each other' I cried bitterly, thinking that I wasn't good enough for them and they were betraying me by making another baby. My mother told me that for years afterwards she was worried I would be scarred for life by the experience of seeing my father jump up naked, ready to punch me.

But she never told me that sex can be for fun, or for pleasure, or that it can be a tool of manipulation, or that it can be a way to mark important moments in your life that have nothing to do with the other person. I had to find all that out for myself. Who it was with the first time wasn't important – it was all about me. I cried afterwards and he thought that he'd hurt me, but they were proud, self-indulgent tears. My mother didn't know for years afterwards; by then her radar must already have started going haywire, because she certainly knew instinctively when I got in the car after my first kiss at a party, my cheeks burning.

I look across at my mother in her bed in the half-light from the streetlamp outside, her head lolling almost off the pillow, drooling slightly, the grooves around her mouth so deep they show even when she's sleeping. I brushed her hair for her before she went to sleep – she likes that; it calms her and she smiles at herself in the mirror and then closes her eyes. I have been sitting in the dark, drinking, not for the oblivion most people seek but because it's the only way I can be emotionally honest. It scares me that I feel so little sometimes, that in the face of sadness I can be so collected. The wine is a relief because it makes me feel human again, if to be human is to be sad.

I don't think my mother was just trying to make me do the right thing by insisting that sex is only about love, I think she genuinely believed it; she lived by that conviction. It must have helped her explain my father's infidelities – they were just about sex, not love, and he always came back to her after a few months, at least until he left her for good, and she went crazy. It wasn't for another woman – that would have made it more bearable for her, to know that he was in love with someone else rather than simply not in love with her. There were other women, of course, but he didn't choose to live with any of them and they came and went like the ebb and flow of tides, and that is what broke her: he chose nothing over her. I didn't pick up for a while just how broken she was, then I came home one day and found my boyfriend holding a pickaxe, looking sceptically at the wall partitioning the lounge from the kitchen, and my mother standing behind him, egging him on, saying the energy in the house was trapped and she had to release it. She made him destroy three walls in the house before my father intervened and checked her into the home. For the first week she didn't once stop crying; the staff here said she cried even in her sleep and her face became so swollen it was unrecognizable to me. Now she is just very quiet – she hardly talks to me, and when she does it is to ask me to do something functional for her: pour a glass of water, brush her hair, put her to bed. She's calm around me and very rarely she takes my hand and strokes it as if she's trying to summon something from the past.

Her head falls suddenly clear of the pillow, onto the mattress, and she begins to snore in her effort to get more air. I walk to the bedside and gently lift her head with two hands, surprised how light it is, full of so many things, so precious, and yet so light, and none of the things she knows were passed onto me. How tiring that you have to start from scratch with each generation when it comes to knowledge, and then by the time you're old enough to want to ask your parents what they know, it's too late: they're mad, estranged or dead. We're always one generation away from barbarism, who said that first? I don't recall. If I imagine having a child myself I feel exhausted at the thought of having to teach it everything I know but haven't even put to good use yet, all these years and years of input and things so painstakingly taught and I haven't done anything with it. I would resent its little gaping mind trying to soak up what I know, absorbing it from me against my will, unless the point of it all is to pass it on, like a baton in a relay, without doing anything fancy with it while it's your turn to sprint. And when I think of what is in my father's head, what kind of carnal knowledge is lodged there, I understand that wiping clean the mind is necessary for survival, for continuation of the species.

My mother didn't feel like that about me; she really wanted to have a child. She loved teaching me things and seeing me grasp at bits of knowledge and fit them together. I was a strange little girl. I talked in tongues for the first four years of my life and my parents had someone come in to observe me; apparently he identified snippets of four different languages that I'd never been taught. I came up with strange theories and experimented with inventions: one theory I had was that fruit flies only bite an apple once, so I hammered a nail into the end of a plank and made a hole in ten apples, believing I could trick the fruit flies into thinking they had already been bitten, but all the apples rotted. I wanted to be a magician for a while, and started at a school for gifted child magicians before the age of ten. My mother encouraged me, and even my father became interested, probably thinking I would boost his own ego by being a child prodigy, but I lost interest after a few lessons, and my father had to force me to keep going, saying one day I would regret giving up. Parents put strange pressures on their children. I remember reading in the newspaper about a little girl whose parents taught her to fly an aeroplane. At age seven she attempted to be the youngest person ever to fly solo across the country; she took off from the city in the middle of a storm and crashed the plane. In interviews afterwards her parents said that she died doing what she loved.

I find it difficult to reconcile tender stories that my mother has told me about my father during my early childhood with my own later memories of his many betrayals. It was a slow process of deflation, a long, tedious, dragged-out series of small disappointments in him that at this stage in my life add up to something substantial. She said the first time they decided to let me cry through the night without feeding me they locked themselves in their bedroom, put their pillows over their heads to dull the sound of me screaming, and both cried for hours, horrified at what they felt they had to do. I have a photograph of him, shirtless and barefoot in a pair of faded jeans, holding me as a tiny baby in the crook of one arm as he vacuums with the other hand; my mother said he would put his music on as loud as it would go and dance around the house with me as he cleaned. Then there's the memory of being in hospital to have my appendix out, and waking after the operation, still groggy, to see the doctor leaning over me, scanning my face, wearing a thick gold necklace that lay flat against her skin; I remember looking at it admiringly, liking how it didn't move even when she bent forward. She saw me looking at it and said, 'Your father gave it to me,' without spite, but without apology. When she stood up I saw that my mother was standing at the door to the room, watching us wearily.

There's another photograph, of the three of us going for a hike and I'm packed into the top of his rucksack and he's look-ing up at me and laughing. And there's the time he took me to the ballet, many years later, and then disappeared backstage to woo one of the dancers when it was over, telling me to wait for him in the foyer, which was full of faded red velvet drapes and upholstery, an attempt at decadence that had failed – bits of it had rubbed right through on the couch, leaving it looking like a diseased dog's coat. As the foyer emptied, the smells of people out for the night (heady perfume, hairspray, soap, mints) faded, leaving behind the damp odour of cigarettes and wine. In boredom, I put my hand down the side of the couch, beneath the cushions, and found a piece of brittle chocolate, a silver coin minted ten years earlier, and an earring studded with stones that shone too brightly not to be fake.

Eventually there was nobody left but me on the couch and a man at the bar, bundled up in a coat and scarf so that his age wasn't apparent – men's faces always look older than their bodies because of cold winds and countless shaves and sports injuries and sunburn. He made eye contact with me and then joined me on the couch. He'd been to see the ballet on his own, he said, because he was in the city on business and leaving the next day. I was unused to male attention then, especially an older man's attention, and I liked how a vein on his temple throbbed when he laughed and how his eyes creased as he talked, and I remember thinking that he would never know how wrinkled his face was because he wouldn't talk to himself in the mirror. I wondered what my face looked like while I was talking. The cleaners began to collect glasses from around us as we spoke. Somebody dropped one on the tiles around the bar and then noisily swept up the shards. A woman began to vacuum directly at our feet and he laughed and suggested we go somewhere more comfortable – to his hotel, just down the block. He didn't ask whom I was waiting for so I didn't tell him. He helped me with my coat and stood aside to let me walk out of the rotating door first. It was snowing outside, the kind of snow that's like flour, fine and dry, and he held my hand as we crossed the road.

At the hotel he poured me a drink while I went to the bathroom. I began to cry, silently, watching myself in the mirror, seeing my face crumple and the colour of my irises intensify with tears. When I re-emerged he was stretching in the small lounge area of the room; he'd taken off his coat and shoes and was bending over and touching his toes in short, rhythmic sets, and I saw immediately that he was too skinny for me – even my shoulders were wider than his – but it was too late at that stage. He stood up, smiling, red-faced from his stretches, and suggested that I take off my shoes and make myself comfortable. I gladly removed my snow boots and took deep sips of the wine he gave me. He looked down at my feet, which were still prune-like from the boots, and said, 'I love that you paint your toe nails. That's so... feminine.' They were hardly painted, the last coat I'd done was months before, and all that was left were some shiny, ragged streaks midway on the nails, showing where they'd grown out. Then he sat down on the bed next to me and began to feel my breasts. When he pushed me back and climbed on top of me he was so light I felt I could lift his whole body with one arm; it was like having a small child lie on me and writhe against my body. I let him do what he wanted to, feeling almost maternal, and when he was done I moved to the other twin bed and fell asleep. In the morning I walked home in the snow and arrived before my father did.

My father didn't hide the evidence of his conquests – in fact, he documented them in a photo album that was kept on a shelf in my parents' bedroom, hoarding them like a trophy hunter adorning his mantelpiece with severed heads. I discovered it one day when I was too young to know what it was, and scribbled with a green crayon on the inside of the cover, but I must have sensed somehow that it would be inappropriate to scribble on the photographs themselves. I would occasionally bring it with me to bed, thinking it was a storybook, and demand that my reluctant father tell me the stories before I went to sleep. Later on, when I began to grasp what it was, it fascinated me differently and I searched for more evidence of the secret lives my parents lived as individuals. In a box with my birth certificate and fading diplomas I found a stack of old love letters they'd written to each other, including something about lying on the bed in the afternoon sunlight and marvelling at each other's bodies, and references to what they'd done the night before. My mother walked into the bedroom while I was reading them and I went bright red and started to cry from the double embarrassment of having read these details and then being discovered doing it. She comforted me and I lied about my tears, saying I was crying because I didn't know if I would ever love anybody like that. She didn't pay the letters much attention – she wasn't nostalgic or sentimental about them – she simply looked at them like long-buried artefacts that have become obsolete, much the same way that she looked at ancient coins in museum display cases.

She would drag me around to museums on school holidays to get new ideas for coin designs. She was Secretary of the Treasury for most of her career, and one of her favourite tasks was working with the State Mint and Bureau of Engraving and Printing to decide on new coin and note designs every five years. It always sounded like a thankless job to me, but she found pleasure in small details, and if you think about it, a brand-new coin or stiffly fresh banknote is a symbol of a state's confidence and power. You hold it in your hand, so shiny or so uncrinkled it looks worthless, and you feel you're holding the evidence that the state is healthy, in order, legitimate. It pleased her to think that each new batch of coins or notes would change hands millions of times, would fuel the economy, would drive human endeavour. She saw the State's currency as the catalyst of all activity in the country and always wished she could track a note to see how many times it was used and reused and for what purposes; often she would examine notes from her purse as if she were hoping to recognize them – the dirtier they were, the better she felt she'd done her job.

I leave the armchair, put the empty wine bottles in the sink and slowly find my way to the bed next to my mother's in the dark. I lie on my side in the bed – I can't sleep on my back – with my right arm cupping my left breast. That's how he lies behind me, my lover, when he feels tender towards me, which is not often. I strain my ears to hear my mother's laboured breathing and the sadness overwhelms me again: I think of lying in my bed as a small child, unable to sleep when my parents had dinner guests because I knew I couldn't call them if I had a nightmare. I could hear them laughing and talking and the music on in the background, and I would lie there rigidly, crying, feeling desperately lonely and helpless and distant from them, even though they were in the next room.

6   *His portraitist's wife*

The fool has chosen to stay here at the Summer Residence even though he's been released along with the others. He woke me from blissful sleep this morning, banging on the door, screaming my name; I thought he was being chased by a pack of wild animals. The guard let him in, and he rushed in on me, threw himself on the bed and said, 'My darling, I'm free,' and immediately started rubbing my belly as if I had a stomach ache. He said they'd given him permission to take me on an outing and he wanted to take me down to the cellars where we went for my birthday, years ago. He'd heard that the vineyard is abandoned now – the owner is too afraid to return – but apparently the stacks of wine bottles are still there and we can help ourselves.

'Not now, obviously,' he said, gazing at my stomach, 'but for later. When things are back to normal.'

It comes as no surprise that I'm being kept on in captivity.

He is looking gaunt and scruffy, but I have to admit there was a thrill of pleasure feeling his body next to mine on the bed. Perhaps it's that I've been starved of physical contact from the outside – on the inside, of course, there is a constant bodily pressure from another being, but it is not enough. The President's wife often suggests she and I should hug more, or give each other neck massages – 'Touch,' she says, 'is healing'

– but I always refuse, saying the baby has made my skin hyper-sensitive and how could I hug her with this belly in the way? She has tried over and over to tell me about her own births – two children, when she was already quite old – in disgusting detail: dilation and fluid and excretions and contractions that I want nothing to do with. Mothers should learn not to ruin it for other women, but she can't help herself, it's her way of possessing childbirth, of making sure I'm on the outside. She does this in other ways, too, usually around money and social standing.

Sometimes she forgets who I am – that I'm not just the por-traitist's wife – and starts pitying me my position. She doesn't know that it's an open secret in my family that the only reason the President married her was because she was wealthy enough not to embarrass him and ugly enough never to humiliate him with another man. My mother is the same age as she is – they were at school together, and their families used to holiday at the same coastal resort. She observed their courtship from close quarters. I think if my mother hadn't stuttered she would have had a chance with the President; stuttering is more shameful than ugliness in their circles, because there's nothing you can do about it. I've worked out that my mother was already preg-nant when she married my father. She was always enigmatic about their wedding date (they've never celebrated anniversa-ries), but I've a way with secrets and I always end up cracking them open like nuts. No wonder they say the truth comes in kernels. She says I was a honeymoon baby. My father was prob-ably just grateful that she had let him be intimate with her and I don't think he thought much about it.

I was ten when the President's son was born. I remember

it vividly because at the resort that summer all the adults expected me to be excited to play with a baby, but instead I almost killed him. My mother walked in on me holding a large toy truck above his cot, ready to crush his skull, but she was strangely sympathetic afterwards, and I recall thinking that I should try it again to elicit similar understanding from her, so I pushed his pram off the veranda, onto the sand below. This time the President saw me do it, and he too was tender with me and didn't tell anyone what I'd done and I wasn't scolded or banished to my room. The baby didn't cry for a week after that and I thought I had done them all a favour. My final experiment was to drop him on his head on the cool concrete floor of the beach cottage: I was holding him, cooing, and then threw him up in the air and pretended to try to catch him on his way down, but let him slip through my hands, slightly breaking his fall. I didn't try anything again after that; even for me the sound of his soft skull hitting the concrete was sickening. He survived these trials, and I watched him closely as he got older, looking for evidence of my experiments, but the only aberration seemed to be that he crawled sideways before he learnt to go forwards. He went on to become a cruelly handsome boy, capable of anything – the thought has occurred to me that the only thing I knocked out of him on the concrete was his moral compass, and that would have been as useful to him as his appendix, or the vestigial nipples on his chest.

The President only asked my father to go into politics when I got engaged to the portraitist. Perhaps he had been worried it would damage my chances of finding a spouse, or attract only the power-hungry like sharks who've smelt their next meal from far off. My father took to it like a fish to water, and transitioned seamlessly from making millions off animals (prawns, horses) to making millions off people (taxes, embezzlement). I had to travel in an armed motorcade to get to my wedding because there was a kidnapping threat at the time – the rebels, and God knows who else, had hit upon the unoriginal idea of taking rich kids hostage and demanding ransom. Sometimes I wonder if my mother would have paid it to get me back.

I was glad to see my husband at the altar, if only because compared to the faces of old boyfriends in the crowd his had not yet collapsed from years of living excessively. It seeps into you, excess, through the pores of your skin like sweat going the wrong way, until you're so bloated you've got only two choices: pop, or float like that until you die; most of us choose to float. One of them propositioned me in the coat room at the reception – his family also bred horses and he had turned out just like one: glossy, sleek-coated, arrogant. Out on the balcony trying to sober up, I bumped into another, and remembered feeling sick the first time I saw his feet – his toes curled like claws and were so uneven I wondered how he could walk, and sex with him was always prickly because he clipped his pubic hair with blunt scissors and it would leave me with a rash on my thighs.

My husband was refreshingly dirty after all these well-groomed men – he purposefully didn't brush his hair while he was at university, and for a while he refused to wear shoes, even in winter (he said he could grip the snow better with bare feet). He marvelled at my ability never to lose my balance on the iced-over roads and pavements, even in high heels. I told him I simply invented a new dance move every time I slipped. I was dancing seriously at the time, as supple as a snake, and my muscles righted themselves effortlessly if I made any sudden movement. He also marvelled at my freckled eyelids and would make me close my eyes under a streetlight in the snow, then kiss the lids, warming the sockets with his breath.

I have tried stretching in the rose garden, but everything feels too tight, and even cross-legged I can barely push my knees to the ground. The President's wife asked me the other day in what position I wanted to give birth and I said on my hands and knees, like a dog, again just to shock her, but she nodded wisely and said that's what she had chosen, so I'm determined now to do it on my back, in the position that started all this in the first place.

One of the benefits of age is that you learn to view your body as an asset instead of an enemy. I would be a better dancer now than I was when I was younger, baby aside. Back then I felt that my narrow shoulders and wide hips made me dance off-kilter, restricted me from true grace because the distribution of my flesh was wrong, and I would bore my eyes into the other dancers who were spindly, the way dancers should be, long and narrow like pencils, trying to find a flaw in their movements. Now I would use my weighted centre to make myself dance like a spinning top; I would do all kinds of things the hipless girls would envy. It would be for the other women, my performance, as most things in a woman's life are. I have never looked at men from my seat in the theatre, or through the car window, or in an elevator, or at a restaurant – I look at the women and they look at me and we rank ourselves constantly according to what we see. In fact, it's a wonder to me that men ever manage to get our attention when we're all so busy looking at each other. In a dancers' changing room you even give up disguising your glances or looks or stares and girls stand next to each other in the full-length mirror and systematically calculate which of them has the better body. The one who loses usually has a prettier face, but that is no consolation.

My husband is outside the door again, waiting for me. I have pulled on a dress and shaken out my hair and brushed my teeth. The guard unlocks the door and once again my husband rushes inside like a puppy and envelops me in an embrace made awkward by my stomach.

'How are we going to get there?' I ask him.

'Your guard will drive us.'

'What is this, a holiday camp?'

He laughs. 'The Commander probably thinks he made a mistake ever taking any prisoners. My theory is that they're keeping you on here for your own good, for our baby's good. We don't know if any of the hospitals are even up and running yet.'

I have my own theories, but I don't share them with him. He takes my hand as we leave the room and strokes it as we walk behind the guard. The Summer Residence is strangely quiet; it seems that most of the party officials have returned to the city, and many of the doors to the rooms are open, with the linen stripped from the beds and in piles on the floor, waiting to be washed. The courtyard is empty.

The car is parked just inside the Summer Residence gates. The guard lets me sit in the front seat and my husband perches in the back, sitting forward on his seat so that our heads are almost in a line. I reach into my handbag and the guard watches me sideways and seems relieved when my hand emerges with my lipstick and compact mirror. Something flits across my husband's face – fear? guilt? – as I apply the lipstick (I can see him behind me in the compact), then the familiar doting look returns and he strokes my shoulder.

The valley spreads below us, revealing more of itself with each turn of the road. I can't see it from my room – my windows face the other way – so it comes as a surprise to remember it's here below the Summer Residence. My family was invited to stay here by the President many times, but my mother always preferred the coast so we never came.

'How are you, my love?' my husband asks, trying to catch my eye in the rear-view mirror. 'How is our baby?'

There is a pleading tone in his voice that betrays him. He still thinks I'm angry at him for putting me in this position, and I will have to play along.

'How do you think I am?' I spit out. 'I'm being held captive, for God's sake.'

He runs his hands through his tangled hair and bites his lip. I look down at the valley again, at the rows and rows of useless vines, untended, unharvested. It will take them years to recover and yield fruit again.

We pass an invisible altitude marker and the air around us thickens perceptibly with heat; even the car seems to feel it and slows down, whining with the effort, and the sweat arrives without warning, making my dress stick to my belly in patches and my thighs cling to the car seat. My husband sweats at his hairline and a dark spot begins to form on his chest; the guard rolls up his sleeves as he drives and I notice that he holds the hot steering wheel with two fingers instead of a whole hand. At the base of the valley he speeds up and the vines fly by us in a green and grey blur. Heat waves have already begun to fuzz the outlines of things, and the farmhouse appears hazily ahead on the road, smaller than I remembered, but the last time we were here we were still in the selfish phase of being in love and anything that we did seemed grand and large and spectacular. We looked down on the people around us, pitying them their loveless existence; my husband talked the owner into taking us down into the cellars which were not open to the public, and he agreed because he envied our love and wanted to be a part of it in any way he could (or so we liked to think).

There is no wind in the valley, so when I leave the car the sweat doesn't dry or cool me down, but makes me more clammy. My husband follows me, after a short, under-his-breath chat with the guard. He must have asked him to stay in the car because the guard sits back down, leaving the door open, lowers his seat-back and stares out at the surrounding fields.

The farmhouse is deserted. Vandals have passed through and gutted it quite neatly, removing everything possible from the walls and floors so that the rooms have a pleasing, empty simplicity. My husband gets onto his hands and knees in the backroom, searching for the ridge in the floorboards that will betray the trapdoor's opening. It is well camouflaged, just like last time – the owner said if we could find the opening he would take us down to the cellars and I fell to my hands and knees to search that time too. My husband finds the ridge and pushes on it to release the catch; it works, and he looks up at me joyfully, then pulls open the trapdoor and drops down into the darkness of the cellar. After a few seconds a dim light appears beneath the floor – he has located the light switch, and his head re-emerges in the hole.

'Don't be afraid,' he says. 'You'll make it – and I'll catch you if you fall.'

I ease myself onto the edge of the hole and then jump forwards into it, but I misjudge the distance and end up knocking him over and landing on top of him, winding him with my stomach. He starts to laugh and wheeze, trying to get breath that his laughter immediately steals from him again. I can't help laughing too, even though my wrist is throbbing painfully. As he writhes and wheezes he keeps holding me on top of him with his arms firmly around my back. Eventually he catches his breath and gazes up at me. I can feel his blood pulsing at various points in his body: at his neck, in his stomach, in his hands. He is warm and soft and he will forgive me for anything. He kisses me, his lips wet from laughing, and after so much time it is almost as exciting as kissing a stranger. I feel desire unfurl in me, starting at the base of my stomach, unobstructed by the baby, shooting around my body.

As I sit up to pull my dress over my head I notice a movement behind one of the barrels, a quick blur of colour that stands out from the pinkish wood. My first thought is cats – they're everywhere in the valley, stray ones; you never see dogs here – but then my heart quickens with anger as I realize it is a human being, hiding behind the barrel, a silent but willing witness. My husband is lying on the cool floor, motionless, smiling with his eyes shut, enjoying the feel of my legs around him. I grip his arm with an urgency that makes him open his eyes, nod with my head to where I can see a shoe sticking out from behind the barrel, and motion to my husband to stay quiet. I lift myself off him and he springs upright, ready to defend me. He tiptoes to the barrel and then throws himself around it onto the intruder. They roll onto the floor, and he manages to pin the man beneath him with his legs, a perversion of the position we were in moments before. The man gives way easily and looks up at us with a familiar face: it's the President's son, the one I dropped on his head as a child.

'What are you doing?' says my husband, bewildered.

'I'm hiding,' he says. 'I've been down here since the coup. I thought nobody would find me here.'

My husband releases him from his grip and leans against a stack of barrels.

'Are you looking for a place to hide?' the son asks scornfully.

'No,' says my husband. The son looks at my face and then down at my belly. He licks his lips. He is holding something behind his back. He licks his lips again, staring at me.

'I know what you did,' he spits at me. His tongue darts in and out of his wet lips.

'What I did, you mean,' my husband says. 'What I did.'

The son lunges at me with a spoke, something he must have pulled from an abandoned bicycle wheel, but I anticipate this and step behind a tower of barrels and push the topmost one. The barrel is empty but heavy enough still to inflict pain when it hits him, crushing his foot, and he slides to the ground and sits cross-legged, cradling his leg, his pulpy flesh held together by the shoe.

My husband makes for the trapdoor opening, pulls a stepladder from the shadows, places it beneath the door, then grabs my hand and tells me to climb. I manage to use my arms to pull myself onto the farmhouse floor and my husband follows, and lets the trapdoor slam shut. Muffled, I hear the son begin to laugh, slow and luxurious laughter, designed to ring in our ears. My husband crawls to where I'm lying on the floor, rolls me over so that our weight is directly above the trapdoor, fits his body into my back, lifts my dress and rubs my stomach in small circles with his free hand. He buries his nose in my nape, inhaling the smell of my scalp, of my faint sweat. He clings to me like an infant animal clutching its mother's fur, as if I were balancing on a tree branch high above the ground, being swayed by the wind, bearing his weight. Is it possible to shake off the child on your back? Would it have dug its claws into your fur too firmly to fall? Would it pull you down with it in its terror?

7 *His barber's brother's fiancée*

My father's hair thinned early. One of my first memories is watching my mother massage olive oil into his scalp, believing – almost religiously, since she did it every evening – that it would slow the relentless retreat of his strands. It didn't, and by the time I was old enough to ride on his shoulders it was difficult to get a grip on his smooth scalp, residually oily from years of massage. I don't think he complained, though: I would watch his face closely while my mother stood above him, thinking it was some kind of ritual that all parents had to perform. He would close his eyes while she kneaded his head, keeping her fingers in one place as she moved his loose skin against his skull. He particularly liked his hairline being rubbed – as it faded, she would move closer and closer up his skull, but at the beginning his hairline was just above his forehead and she had to stand in front of him to get traction. The reverse ritual was that my father shaved my mother's armpits for her; she said if she tried to do it herself she nicked the soft skin from not being able to see the blade. She would sit in the bath and he would crouch on the bathmat next to her, lather her armpit hollows and then hold each arm up in the air in turn as he slid the razor gently along her contours.

At breakfast today the chef insisted that we discuss the

menu for the weekend at length, in private. My husband smirked at me across the table – he likes to watch the chef desiring me, he says – then finished his eggs and strode out of the dining room with that open-legged gait of his that is beginning to seem like a deliberate showcasing of his crotch, forcing people to acknowledge before anything else that he is a man, and a virile one at that. Last night I tried to delay getting into bed until he was asleep, but he was waiting for me like a crab in its lair, and dragged me into an embrace before I could stop him. It is terrifying that desire can rot into disgust, and so quickly too; it makes me deeply suspicious of my brain, that it could mislead me so willingly in the past, make me crave his hand pressing on my breast or probing my thighs. I wonder if all people consciously put themselves under a man or woman's spell, and if the necessary precursor to desire is a blocking out, a suspension of disbelief, an overlooking of the things about that person that – when the spell is broken – make you wonder how you ever desired them at all. The spell can be broken even after somebody has died. When my husband first touched me, only months after my fiancé – the barber's brother – had been buried, I was surprised he did not smell of fish. The spell was broken: I wondered how I had put up with fish-scales in my bed, on my skin, the fish-oil scent of my pillows, the salt in his hair. I must remember this, that one day I will look back at the barber and wonder how I could ever have touched him.

The chef followed me onto the balcony, where strong wind in the night had pulled a small palm from its pot. I knelt to pick it up and scoop the soil from the tiles and he knelt beside me, too close to me. His eyes searched for my scars greedily, then he took my arm and turned it to reveal the puckered circles, six of them. In the morning light the skin looked worse than usual, dark and purplish.

'I brought something for these,' he whispered. 'It will help them heal.'

Without letting go of his grip, he used his other hand to dip into his apron, removing a small glass bottle filled with oil. I tried to pull away, but he gripped more tightly.

'It will make them feel better,' he whispered.

I began to get to my feet, desperate to wrench my arm free, and then his voice changed its tenor; it was no longer beseeching.

'I know what you did,' he whispered, slightly out of breath from the effort of holding me. 'What you're doing.'

I stopped struggling. He tentatively let go of my arm and I did not move it; it lay leaden on his lap, the scars on the inside of my forearm exposing themselves to him. He rubbed oil slowly onto them, anointing me, then he let me go. I did not know where else to go but to him, to the barber.

This time I ignore my own reflection in his shop window, where, glued to the outside of the cracked glass, is one of the posters the Party has pasted up throughout the city, on my husband's orders. It cannot be coincidence. I have not seen this photograph before, this particular pattern of damage done to a face; it is his face – my fiancé, the barber's brother – it is his face, but who would want to recognize it like this, who would want to attach themselves to it in any way? My husband must have hidden it from me, this photograph; he claimed there was no documentation of his death, that at least this small mercy had been granted. It is freshly applied, the glue is still wet in places, making bits of the poster translucent. I pull at the edge, hoping it will glide off smoothly, but it sticks and the thin paper tears. I put my face against the glass to peer inside. It is dark and empty, he is not yet here. Where did he say he lived? I don't think he told me. I begin to scratch at the poster with my fingernails, ripping long shreds of it away from the glass, but not enough; it refuses to come off. A group of men further down the street look at me suspiciously, huddle more closely together, surveying the debris that surrounds them, littered down the street from the riots. I look around me frantically, spot across the street an abandoned chair with sturdy iron legs and force it against the glass; the existing crack sends out shoots, but doesn't yield.

Somebody above me begins to shout and, afraid, I look up. It's the barber, standing on a ledge above the shop, sleepiness banished by the violence of what I'm doing. He disappears, probably running to get downstairs to stop me. I swing the chair against the glass again and it varicoses but holds. Then he is next to me, and gently takes the chair from me, and folds me into his arms, my head turned away from the window. I feel his body stiffen as he sees the poster, but he holds me against him still.

'Go upstairs,' he says. 'The stairs are through the back room.'

I obey him, tired of my own rage, and walk through the shop without looking back, aware of the bulbs fizzing around the mirror, and through the backroom where the bottled hair seems to press against the glass like large, captive spiders. Halfway up the stairway I hear the window shattering, throwing its splinters to the pavement, releasing the poster from its grip.

The barber's room is small but ritualistically tidy. He must have made his bed after leaping from it only seconds ago; despite the urgency with which he must have known he had to act, he still managed to pull the cover straight, to flatten the pillows. The spices stacked against the wall beside the sink are colour-coded: from chilli to turmeric to saffron, down to the blue-tinged pepper. His belts are rolled into tight circles and propped in circular plastic holders, specially designed for the purpose. I pull open a drawer to find underwear folded neatly into perfect squares. Only now, seeing this, do I realize how the state of the shop downstairs must bother him, must eat away at his desire for order. I wonder if my body is pure enough for him, if my laxity about certain things bothers him, if he has to will himself not to pull my dress straight or untwist my stockings when I leave him, looking dishevelled, after we've been together.

'I didn't want you to see this,' he says quietly, behind me, standing in the doorway. 'The way I live. I thought it might scare you, put you off.'

I swallow and close the drawer. 'You must have your reasons,' I respond. 'I'm only afraid I might not be clean enough for you. Not well ordered.'

He buries his face against my neck. 'You purify me,' he whispers into my hair. 'You are my salve.'

'As in salvation?' I whisper back.

He doesn't respond, but carries me to his bed and lays me upon it and the thought runs through my mind: I am an offering on a pyre, a sacrifice, soon I will go up in flames. He removes my dress, his own shirt. I notice his hand is bleeding, dripping blood onto his pristine bed cover; he notices my scars

145

are inflamed, an angry crimson, and oily as if oozing. He kisses them softly, tastes the oil.

'It's just a balm,' I say quietly, in justification. 'A poultice.'

The face of his brother, of my fiancé, hovers above us like an apparition. I think of the poster torn to shreds by the shattered glass, or perhaps the pieces have clung to its back, a limp, heavy mosaic. The barber will want some proof that it is not his brother I'm imagining against my body. What can I give him this time, what small offering? I will give him possession, give him pity for his loss.

'I'm so sorry about your brother,' I whisper as he unclasps his belt.

Not my fiancé, but his brother. Put his loss first, dim my own, and hope he believes me, and it is true, at least for now: it is his face I want beside my own, his chest against my back, his feet curled beneath mine. He cries; it worked.

Before I leave, I ask to see my jar of hair again. He is dubious, worried that I find it perverse, but he does not remember that I, too, am a hoarder, or perhaps his brother never told him about my treasure-hunting. I appreciate this instinct in him, the urge to sweep up strands and bottle them; I would have taken it even further and transformed them into something: a woven floor-mat, a curtain tie-back, a wig. I am surprised to feel jealous of the women's hair that he has collected that is not mine – it gives itself away because the long hair coils against the jar; the men's is short and stacked. He hands me my jar and I pull out a single thick hair: how strange that this was loosened from my scalp in the course of silent desire, not wanting to wake his mother and brother, and forgotten on the pillow for this man beside me to collect the next morning in his foraging. My fiancé went grey from the shock of being captured in the mountains – surely a fibre that can change its own colour is alive? Why does wet hair freeze as hard as an icicle in the winter, but does not snap in two? Why do strands jingle against each other like metal if they are dead?

'Do you remember,' I say to him, 'the bits of china in the dry earth around your house?'

He looks suddenly shifty, worried that I will forsake him for the memory of his brother.

'I never knew how old they were, if they were newly dumped or had been exposed by the wind after many years,' I continue. 'I collected some of them. I once managed to piece together a whole tea cup with a delicate handle.'

He relaxes; he sees I am simply confessing my own taste for collecting.

'I saw one of your rubbings once,' he says shyly. 'My brother showed me. It was a life-sized silhouette of a knight with crest and armour. From an old gravestone.'

The thrill of making those! Stealing into churches in the late afternoons, before the bustle of evening service, with a roll of cheap paper and a hunk of charcoal, and rubbing away like my life depended on it. The lines at first didn't make sense and I would despair, but gradually the details appeared, filling out the figure: a breastplate, a spear, a scroll, pointed metal foot armour. My hands and face were black when it was done. The church disapproved, of course – they said it was equivalent to desecration – but I had each one framed and hung above my bed.

'And your cowrie shells, he showed me those too.'

Smooth and tight as a baby's fist.

The barber kisses me goodbye; watches me leave from the backroom. The shop is draughty now. I step through the empty window instead of using the door. On my way back to the Residence, along the seafront promenade that leads right into the Presidential District, I collect things, my scavenging instincts reawakened. It is calming, the slow process of perusal, and the streets are full of treasure overlooked by looters. The whole city has been turned into a rubbish tip to dig through; the sandy soil has been forced to loosen its clutches on the bits and pieces that have sunk into it over the years and disappeared. The concrete slabs along the seafront have been shattered, the shards push against each other like tectonic plates, revealing soiled underbellies. In one recess I find a glass bottle with the stopper intact. It is green like ice in evening light, soft and cloudy from being rolled by the sea. I wish impulsively there was a note inside it, but of course there isn't, just a faint sweetness like an old woman's perfume. The base of the bottle is thick, sturdy: glass and tar are liquid, they thicken at the bottom over time. Women too.

Beside the railing overlooking the sea, I see a folded baby's pram, the old-fashioned kind with four wheels and a hood. It is upholstered in corded velvet, the pile still plush but drenched by the sea. I unfold it with force – the salt has already begun to rust the joints – and find inside the carriage a thin mattress and fronded blanket. What are babies' heads meant to smell like? Mothers always say their napes smell milky, distinctive, like a puppy's breath, addictively sweet. I would not know. If I were to give birth in nine months' time, I would not know who the father was. Would a different father mean a different nape-scent?

I think about what the barber asked me when we lay together in his bloodied bed, the cover dirty and twisted. I could
sense him restraining himself, forcing himself to let the pillow
lie skew on the floor, to leave his clothes in a tangled puddle.
He asked about my husband, 'the Commander', he called him.
Was I in love with him? What did I see when I looked at his
face? I told him the truth, that I'm afraid of him, that I've been
afraid for some time now, even before the coup. I had not seen
the President's face up close until he was captured and put
in a room in the Summer Residence, and when I saw him for
the first time I saw my husband as he will be when he is an
old man: haggard, greedy, lustful. At first his zealousness was
attractive, but now, months after the coup, I have learned to pay
attention to what he is a zealot about, and sadly, it seems it is
as unoriginal as power. In turn, I asked the barber what makes
him feel so dirty, so tainted. 'What do you think?' he replied,
without archness.

I leave my hoary treasures at the base of the stairs in the City
Residence. As I climb the stairs I think about the lake on the far
northern border of the country, where I have always wanted to
go. Legend has it there is a plane, a bus and also a helicopter
at the bottom, all from tragic accidents, now slowly growing
barnacles. A scavenger's dream. I let myself into my bedroom
cautiously, as if expecting someone to be waiting for me. The
shades are drawn and my eyes adjust slowly. Across the bed
– my side of the bed – someone has draped the same poster that
I have beneath my fingernails, the head perfectly positioned
on my pillow. I know my husband did this; his descent into
tyranny has begun. I run to retch into the toilet bowl and find
the lid is up; another man has been here, has lifted the lid to

piss. Behind me in the mirror I see the chef, and I know what he has come for, and what knowledge he has to make me give it to him. He starts by kissing my inner arm slowly, one kiss for each scar.

8 *His chef's daughter*

On their own, in isolation, each of my facial features is acceptable: if I cover my nose and mouth with my hands and stare only at my eyes, I see two perfectly fine ovals looking back at me, one could even call them sultry. If I cover my nose and forehead and stare at my lips, they are bud-like, fleshy, pink. But taken all together something is not right; as an ensemble my face is a failure, and it will only get worse with time. For a fancy-dress party a few months ago I drew exaggerated black lines in the corner of my eyes to make them seem feline, but the effect instead was an anticipation of crow's feet and it surprised me to realize that I will become even uglier as I age. Standing at the basin brushing my teeth, I glance down at my pale, stocking-sheathed feet and think, this is what they will look like when I am dead.

The bill has still not been paid, and yesterday the manager told me he would have to kick out my mother if he does not receive payment by the end of the month, so I'm finally forced to go searching for my father at the Residence. I'll have to pretend to be looking for work as a kitchen girl so I can at least get into the kitchens and find out if he's still there. I kiss my mother's forehead goodbye: she has dried food around her mouth and her chin is gristly with the beginnings of old woman's whiskers. I can't bear to watch her eat anymore – the sound is the worst part of it, the damp mastication. Last night she somehow got food on one of her eyebrows and in her hair. All of a sudden, I have a strong urge to suck my thumb, to find a spot on my pillow that smells gamey (of my scalp and spit and night breath) and lie with my nose against it and my thumb against the backs of my front teeth. Childish impulses, but perhaps it is from being around my mother for too long: she has reverted, so why shouldn't I?

I walk towards the Presidential District, wondering if it will be renamed. Already it is hot and dry outside; days like this remind me of the story my mother always used to tell, of drying my freshly washed but still damp nappies in seconds by holding them outside the window of a moving car in the dead-heat of midday. It is early; the city streets are empty except for the men at the roadblocks, who lounge on the pavements smoking and make sucking sounds when I cross onto the other side of the street to avoid them. They are armed – their trousers bulge with their weapons. I regret wearing stockings in this heat, they scratch at the sweaty parts, at the backs of my knees, my feet, at the small of my back. I veer towards the seafront for the relief of the cool air off the sea. The Residence looms above the city from its perch at the summit of the hill. I used to be able to see it from my bedroom window in our last house and at night it would glitter with the hundreds of camera flashes fired off by tourists visiting for the view of the city lights from the top; all those photographs of the same thing, so many albums stuffed with the same memento.

The paragliders are up already, throwing themselves off the hill into the morning thermals, hovering about the rocky outcrops like giant butterflies. Every time I see them I almost will them to fly into the rockface or land in the sea, just to know what it would look like. I once climbed up to the ledge they jump off and suddenly came eye to eye with one of them – he, a human cocoon, hovering, airborne, and me, landlocked; it was like coming face to face with an alien creature. Things must be back to normal if they're out again – they are like weather vanes that way; their launching place is closed off to them in times of stress, to keep people away from the Residence. The sea is two-toned and calm this morning, and the line marking the edge of the reef is crisp. Cats twine around each other at the rubbish bins along the seafront, one lurches out of a bin as I pass. The sea has washed away some of the debris left here after the looting, and the pavement is wet and dark with bits of coagulated rubbish stuck against the wall keeping out the sea.

I am longing for my lover, the President's son, as usual, craving him guiltily, and to stave off my longing I pinch the thin skin above my knuckles with my fingernails until it bleeds. It is the places that are usually never touched that can generate unexpected pleasure, mostly just from the surprise of it: heels, the flesh between thumb and forefinger, the front-side of a thigh, the inside of an elbow, pressure put on the half-moon of a fingernail. They can also generate unexpected pain, but I can no longer tell the difference. I could blame him, of course, but it would be like blaming God for creating me, for giving me this face, these legs, this stomach. I prefer to blame my father. He is, after all, the one who gave me a taste for cruelty – although he likes to inflict and I have been trained to endure. I can't bear to think of my lover holed up somewhere, in hiding, without me.

Where could he have run to? I would know if he were dead; it would be sweet release and despair.

He is five years older than me and was still a child himself when it all began. We were in the room at the Summer Residence with the framed puzzle of a dignitary on the wall – the pieces fitted tightly, but still the man's face seemed cracked from the hundreds of slotted joinings. We lay together on the floor of the room – there was no furniture, or it was covered with sheets – and stared up at the picture, which bothered me: why was it a puzzle and not simply a painting? I wanted to get behind the glass and pull the smirking face apart into its constituent pieces; no matter how much to the left or right I moved, the eyes followed and fixed me with their stare. I could feel his skin against mine, our arms touching, and I tried to match his breathing – I held my breath until he breathed out, then waited for him to breathe in again. He took my hand and squeezed it very tightly, so tightly I gasped, then he told me to follow him.

He kept squeezing my hand all along the corridor, across the courtyard, through the sculpture garden, and to the base of a thickly leaved, spreading tree growing closely against one of the bottom windows of the Summer Residence. He told me to climb the tree, but my fingers were numb from being gripped and I fell and shaved off a fine layer of skin against the bark. He laughed and pushed me against the trunk again, ordering me to climb. I managed to claw my way up and onto a branch, my new wound burning, desperate to please him. He lifted himself onto the branch next to me and cautiously parted the leaves so that we could see into the room through the window without being seen ourselves. At first I could see nothing but the reflection of the tree in the glass, then I saw something white moving inside the room, some kind of animal, and the animal separated into two, and I realized it was an entwined mass of naked human flesh. The President's face came in and out of view as the mass rolled; the woman I did not recognize. I was transfixed by the violence of what they were doing. The President's son moved his leg against mine on the branch. His breath was hot against my cheek, his breathing quickened as he watched.

'I watch him often,' he whispered. 'He likes to hurt many women. He thinks nobody knows.'

A strange ticking began in the base of my stomach, a nervous pulsing, and I began to feel thirsty. The son put his mouth against my neck and bit me slowly, clenching his teeth tighter and tighter until I yelped. Then he put one hand between my thighs and with his other he dug a fingernail into the open wound on my knee, keeping his eyes on the moving flesh inside the window. If I strained my ears hard enough, I could hear the woman inside moaning from pain. I tried to be silent, proud of my resilience, proud that he wanted to hurt me. It felt good.

It still feels good; he is still my lover. I feel guilty because now I know that pain and pleasure are not meant to be paired, but it is too late to unlearn it, it has been burnt into my brain, gouged into my body. I have tried to resist him, but it is useless. In a drought, wild animals are driven mad by thirst and swarm to the sea against their instincts, drink sea water and then die a horrible death, leaving the beach littered with their bodies. I am perpetually mad with thirst for him; without him I will go even madder.

In the thick of the Presidential District the debris is denser and there are the same gruesome posters plastered against walls and windows and even nailed into trunks. The avenue slopes up towards the gated entrance to the Residence, cano-pied by jacarandas. I approach the security booth with my best schoolgirl walk, looking innocent and apprehensive while the sweat threads its way down my back. The guard is on edge, his radio buzzes with barked commands that I can't decipher, but he swallows my story and radios the kitchens to ask a busboy to fetch me at the gate. While I wait he shifts from foot to foot, looks at his watch nervously, and glances at my legs. I notice my stockings have laddered badly up the back of my knee and beneath my skirt. We wait in silence punctuated by men's quick shouted orders on his radio.

The busboy leads me through the gate and across the lawn towards the kitchen garden and then through a service entrance into the dishwashing gulley where three men stand side by side hosing food scraps off plates. One of them sees me and nudges the young boy to his side, and they both whistle and grunt at me as I pass. The busboy tells me to wait in the gulley while he fetches somebody who will interview me for a job. 'Nothing fancy going,' he says, 'just peeling duty and the dishes.' I peer through the porthole window in the swinging door into the kitchens. The room is steamy and filled with men dressed in white with plastic caps over their hair and bright red faces; with all the banging and clanging it sounds like a factory assem-bly line. My father would not be back here, though, unless to scream at somebody in fault.

I clear my throat and shout at the dishwashers above the noise of the plates being piled in the sink, 'Who is executive chef now?'

The oldest man, wrinkled as a walnut, hears me and shouts back, 'Same as before.'

Relief flows into my blood and through my veins, not just for my mother's sake, but for my own. I have missed him, despite myself, I am still his little girl. I knew he would survive.

A harassed man pushes at the swinging door wildly, spots me and says, 'Start tonight, trial week.'

I turn to him and say coldly, 'I'm not looking for work. I'm looking for my father.'

Even this man must see the resemblance because he looks suddenly terrified and his eyes dart from my eyes to my jaw-line and back. The dishwashers have turned off their hoses to listen and now stand staring at me, their hands pink from the hot water.

'He's not here now,' the man manages deferentially. 'You can wait in the lobby, I'll tell him you're here.'

He points through the service door to the main entry to the Residence, where guards bristle on the stairway. All four men watch me walk away across the gardens and towards the stairs. I take them two at a time and get to the top out of breath. The guard seems to think I'm a servant because he pays me no attention – I suppose he saw me leave the kitchens – so I walk through the door and into the quiet, carpeted lobby, and sit on a chair with a leather studded seat in a dark corner and fold my legs.

From here I can see into the dining room on my left and into a large meeting room (long reflective wooden table, important chairs) on my right. This is the official part of the Residence, the part that is for public living. The curving staircase before me leads to the bedrooms and bathrooms and reading rooms tucked away from scrutiny on the next floor. At the base of the stairs is a small pile of what looks like debris – a folded pram and a plastic packet bulging with junk; the cleaners must not yet have thrown it away. Who is living here now? I haven't followed the papers; I don't even know who organized the coup. Who sleeps in the President's bed? Does he have a wife?

The lobby is so quiet I can hear faint sounds of metal being sharpened, crockery being piled, a man shouting a joke, from the kitchens behind the dining room. My curiosity wells like strong hunger. Even though I know nobody is in the room, I look around me suspiciously and over my shoulder and around the corner as far as I can see. Then I stand quickly and walk up the stairs confidently, like I'm meant to be there. I can always say I got lost – first day on the job, that kind of thing. Although if my father's relationship with the last President is anything to go by, he will probably be a solid favourite already and able to talk his way out of anything, even his daughter snooping around the Residence. After days cooped up in the home with my mother, I wouldn't mind a little adventure – I've always liked to see the earthly trappings (underwear on the floor, toothbrush in the basin, tabloid on the bedside table) of people in power, probably as a result of what I saw through the window with the President's son in the tree. It becomes addictive.

The stairs are carpeted and muffle my steps. I remember the way to the bedroom from the time the President's son gave me the grand tour of the Residence while his parents were out and we lay on a bed and he pretended to be his father (distorted his eyebrows, scrunched up his mouth) and lay on top of me, suffocating me until I kicked him to get a breath of air, then begged him to cover me again. There were foundation stains on one of the pillows, and on the sheets halfway down the bed there were cryptic stains, vaguely oily.

I walk along the corridor, keeping to the wall, counting the doors. At the third door on my right I stop: this is the bedroom. Of course he won't be in there now, it is mid-morning and he'll be out on official duties or doing whatever a new President does. The door is cracked open; maybe the maid is in there cleaning. The room is dark and empty; the blinds are still drawn but they flutter in the wind from the open sliding door onto the balcony. I push tentatively on the door and step inside the room. There is a poster draped across the bed – one of the mangled body ones – and clothes on the floor next to the door leading to the bathroom. Suddenly I hear a sound from the bathroom, a low whine like a dog in distress. I walk quickly across the room and out onto the balcony. The President's son showed me a way to look into the bathroom from outside without being seen. I reach up to the air vent and remove the lid carefully, and put my eye to the gap.

9   *His portraitist's wife*

Before I realized I was pregnant I was perturbed by a spate
of strange shooting pains in different bones around my body
– shins, spine, collarbone. Afterwards, when I was told I was
expecting, I began to suspect that the pains were from the child
gathering material for itself, leeching nutrients from me, digging deep into my bones to nourish its own. I also believed it
was digging for something else, for knowledge of my own pain-
ful memories, deposits left by anger, pathways forged by fear, so
that it could collect them and soak them up and thereby spare
itself the pain of having to make its own mistakes. I resented its
assumption that it could get away with it and sidestep misery
so easily.

I want it out of me; I am sick of my lumbering, side-to-
side shuffle that passes for a walk; I am tired of my swollen
ankles and the dark stain down the centre of my stomach and
the mask around my eyes and the incessant need to piss and
waking myself with my own snoring because this baby is pushing something against my lungs and suffocating me. In the
sculpture garden I still try to stretch, but it has become a comic
routine so now I am simply walking in slow circles around the
rose bushes. Glancing down, I notice a strange plant I haven't
seen before – a single glossy-green leaf like a sow's ear pushed

flat against the soil. I pull it out of the ground and find that its roots are surprisingly shallow and wispy. It reminds me of the desert up north where the winds are so strong the trees have grown with their trunks almost flat against the ground. I always found their prostration distasteful – it seemed to me the ultimate concession, literally bending over backwards to accommodate a stronger force. A cat lurks against the garden wall, rubbing itself against the bricks and I call it to me cheerfully, entice it closer, and then hit its flank as hard I can with the flat of my hand. It squawks and skitters away and over the wall. An old childhood trick I learned from my mother (she always preferred dogs).

I keep catching myself thinking about her against my will, probably because I'm about to become a mother myself, and the only model I have for this process is her. I dreamed last night that I had caught her stutter like a common cold and all the men I spoke to looked at me at first with pity and then not at all. This morning I woke with an extremely clear image of her in my mind, hovering above me at the beach with her face very close to mine, digging me into a sand motor car. And I could have sworn I caught a whiff of her night perfume in the garden just now, close to the wall, but then I saw the camellias growing thickly around the tap. She would come to kiss me goodnight before she and my father went out and I would hear her high heels clicking on the polished parquet and smell her scent before she'd even opened the door. Freshly bathed, in my nightgown, I would beg her not to go, or make her promise to kiss me again when she arrived home at the end of the night, and I told her I would know even if I was sleeping because she could kiss my cheek and I would find the lipstick mark in the morning. I never found a mark, but I would console myself that it had simply rubbed off onto my pillows in the night, or she had wiped it off herself after kissing me, not wanting to soil the linen.

And lately I have had the urge to be back at work, for the small, quiet frivolity of it, the open-faced superficiality, the detailed deception. I am tired of the burden of bearing another human being, the enforced earnestness of impending mother-hood. I want to lather a square box with shaving cream and call it a cake, and dye a glassful of water with food colouring and call it wine, and put a chunk of dry ice at the bottom of a bowl of rice and call it steam. I'd like to paint grapes with clear nail varnish or cut chips out of polystyrene or spray moisture beads onto the side of a can. At work I mastered the art of show-ing no expression, appropriate given my vocation. I cultivated a habit of leaving a long pause before I answered any questions. The people I worked with gave me respect because of it, and because of who I am (or who my family is); they had a healthy respect for power and the privilege it confers.

The guard whistles for me to return to my room and it is a relief to sink into the bed and lift my feet onto the bedpost to try to drain the fluid from them. Even as a dancer my feet never hurt this much, this consistently, although I had terrible bunions growing like bulbs out of the sides of my feet and my nails would ooze after a big performance. I have started to crave space – this room is not exactly small, but as I've ballooned the ceiling has begun to bother me; it hangs so low and solid above me. I've been longing for my first apartment in the city, the one my father bought for me to live in at university – it was one of the city's oldest buildings and had somehow survived despite being surrounded by slick new skyscrapers. There was a balcony from every sprawling room and high, canopied ceilings. I hung beads from doorways and painted the doors aquamarine and always had bowls of nuts and strange fruit lying around on side tables and window sills. I made one of the rooms into my studio – I lined the walls with mirrors and installed a long wooden bar along one side. With the doors onto the balcony open I could see directly into one floor of a glassed-in office block, the kind with fluorescent lighting and air conditioning no matter what the weather: a sterilized climate all year round. Men in suits would stand with their faces to the glass at lunchtime to watch me perform. When the dance was over, sweaty and heaving, I would look directly at them, acknowledge their presence. Some looked forlorn, others made obscene gestures, a few pressed their phone numbers writ large to the window.

There is a knock at the door and the President's wife calls in her pearly-bright voice, 'I'm coming in!' The guard rolls his eyes at me before he closes the door behind her and locks it. She looks about her and pats her bushy hair and walks towards me shaking her head.

'My poor dear,' she says. 'Let me give you a massage.'

Before I can move my legs she has sat down on a chair next to the bed, swung my feet down into her lap and begun to roll my left ankle while gripping the heel with her other hand.

'And how was your little outing with your husband?' she asks coyly, winking at me while she milks my foot like an udder. 'I loved being... intimate when I was pregnant, especially with the first,' she says suggestively when I don't answer. 'It made me feel so feminine, so rounded and, well, desirable, you know?'

She lifts my right foot entirely off her lap and begins to bang her palm against the heel, over and over. 'But the stretchmarks are going to be horrendous. You'll have to work hard to keep him interested.' She tugs at each toe in turn, until the tiny bones click. Then she threads her fingers through the spaces between my toes and jiggles them violently.

'There's something I need to tell you,' I say. 'I wanted to wait until we were released but who knows when that will be.'

She is delighted at the promise of a confidence, and leans close towards me so that my feet push into the folds of her belly, licks her lips and says, 'Oh, tell me.'

'It's about your son,' I say, then pause and look out of the window wistfully. I will make her wait; I intend to enjoy her suffering. Her grip has become vice-like around my ankles and her eyes are bulging slightly.

'He's...'

I pause again and look down at my hands, then adjust my dress over my stomach, pulling on it to undo the creases.

'Your son is dead. I saw his body at the vineyard.'

She falls forward onto my outstretched legs, clings to me about my knees, and sobs and moans and wails until the guard opens the door to see about the noise. He quickly closes it again at the sight of her thrashing about with grief. Her make-up drools onto my dress and my bare legs, but I can't find the right moment to pull them away. Eventually she lifts her head, keeping her arms around my knees, and looks at me with her melted face.

'Oh, you poor thing,' she sobs. 'You don't even know it is your loss too.'

My loss? Does she intend that in the patriotic sense, that we have all lost a good 'son' of the country? I pat her head, reassuring her that no, it is most definitely her loss. She becomes impatient, and lets go of my legs and sits up.

'There's something I should tell you now,' she says, sniffling, her mascara blurred like a black eye. She grips my feet again, pulls at my big toes nervously. 'He was…' She breaks down and weeps again.

I begin to feel alarmed, backed into an enclosure like an animal fattened for the kill.

'He was your half-brother. You have lost your half-brother.' She moans loudly and pulls at her hair.

'But the President?' I whisper incredulously. She watches me closely, despite her tears.

'He's your father,' she whispers back. 'We thought it was best for you not to know. I promised your mother I would never tell you.'

My insides contract into a breathless, timeless point of agony and then, just as suddenly, the pain is gone. She puts her hand to my stomach, but I don't want her to touch me anywhere, I can't bear her cloying fingers on me, and I push them off violently and kick at her to let go of my legs. Before I can stand up the white-hot pain paralyses me again and I squat on the floor and dig my nails into my knees to wait it out. In that time she manages to come around to me and crouches beside me, stroking my hair.

'It's starting,' she says. 'The baby.'

As soon as the pain is gone I stand and run towards the door and hurl my fists against it, screaming to the guard to open it. As he opens the door, there is a liquid flush and suddenly I'm standing barefoot in a pool of water. He looks with horror down at my feet and then at my drenched dress and turns his face away. The President's wife hobbles to me and screams at the guard, 'Get somebody, can't you see she's going to have the baby!' and he disappears gratefully, sprinting down the corridor. I push her aside against the post of the door, hoping that she will hit her soft head on the hardwood, but at that instant the pain debilitates me and I squat again by instinct to ease it and clench my eyes and ball my fists. She is still there when it passes and just the sight of her face makes me nauseous; I want to hurl out the contents of my stomach, of my entire body, leave them in a slop on the floor and peel off my skin like a cooked beetroot. And then I will be nothing but a membrane for things to pass through.

Oh mother, you win. I underestimated you. You have a taste for deception, a taste I have inherited. How did it happen? Where were you? In the dunes? Beside the reservoir at midnight? On a blanket beneath the power lines? Did you feel your spine against the warm hood of his car on an abandoned road? Did you stutter when you whispered to him your desires, instructions, preferences? It was not love – I know that he is incapable of it. Did his hands look different when he was young? Were his fingers more agile, more insistent? Oh, the great art of it, the sidling up to father afterwards, reeking of another man. Did you lock your jaw stoically when you had to let father touch you to take the credit, the responsibility, ownership of me? No wonder he always examined my face under the lamp. He wasn't marvelling at my unscarred skin, he was sniffing like a suspicious dog around a lamp-post, trying to figure out which was his piss and which was someone else's, and whether I could be taken for granted as his territory. He was always gratified by my face – did he not see the strange size of my eyes or the foreign slope of my cheekbones? But his own face had been disfigured for too long for him to remember the geography of his own features, and there were always photographs of long-forgotten ancestors that could be brought out to account for these little discrepancies.

I run into the sculpture garden with my thighs gliding smoothly against each other and my wet dress clinging to my legs. She follows me, tries to pull me back by my shoulder, but I slap her hand away and then I'm bent over again with the pain, the terrible wait, the anguish, a pain that banishes all sense of time. It passes – how long did it last? – and I realize she is rubbing my back, kneading my spine through my dress. I lash out at her sideways and keep running, searching, my eyes focused on the ground, warding off the next spasm of pain, trying to take as many heavy steps forward before it attacks again.

We were on the deck, night-time, salt on the air. Corn on the cob. A dropped fork. We were in the forest behind the Residence in the dark. A monogrammed towel filched from the laundry closet. Someone lurking behind a tree nearby, watching. A desperate sprint away. A photograph left under my pillow. To provoke me, to invoke his power, to stir our desire. Sausage-spotted face above me, wrinkles, discolouration, panting. The President's sagging belly, bandy legs. His old man's hands. The aftertaste of submission. His terrifying ascendance.

I see the shears lying in the grass ahead of me. If I can just get there before the pain cripples me, but no, it hits again, a solid wall of it, and I crouch and dig my hands into the soil. When I open my eyes she is beside me again, and now there are men, and they see me staring at the shears and quickly they are removed, and here's my husband running towards me, damn fool, and the guard is holding him back and he's screaming. As though he knows what pain is. I will be dragged somewhere and will have to force it out. Perhaps there is another way to do it; I could hold back and not push when I'm supposed to and starve it of oxygen and keep its dirty soft skull lodged in me. Two guards hook their arms beneath my armpits and the President's wife tries to hold my legs but I kick at her and manage to connect with her chin. She reels backwards, holding her face. Before the next contractions shunt me into oblivion I glimpse the almost-black blood streaming from her split chin.

I should have known. He was a sick old man. Sick old men don't just like young women – that wasn't it after all. They like a little something extra, a bit of a twist, a cherry on top of their perversion. I hear a man shouting far off in the distance, and a woman howling faintly a long, long way away; there is a terrible weight in my head and on my eyes and a heaviness and fading.

PART III

1 *His barber*

I have been summoned again, this time to the Residence on the hill, and now he wants to try something new: a lather and shave. It seems he trusts me enough to put a knife to his neck. I soak the blades in peroxide, sharpen them against each other, unwrap a new block of shaving soap from wax paper, trim the shaving brush of its matted ends, and put three drops of camomile oil in a bottle of distilled alcohol to dab at his cheeks and neck while they are still raw from the shaving. My assistant fusses around me with clean towels and a plastic apron. He is particularly clingy today and keeps asking me when I will be back, what time he should expect me, and should he keep me some supper? I ignore him, but kindly – he has not been the same since I was taken away and he had to hide from the looters in the backroom. I am thankful they could not force their way through and up into my bedroom; I could not deal with any more disorder. Just before I leave, I hold the tweezers in the open flame of a match to disinfect them in case the Commander wants his ear or nostril hair pulled.

The district is quiet. It is the time of day when the heat makes movement uncomfortable and people close their windows because the air trapped inside kitchens and dark bedrooms from the morning is cooler than the hot wind now blowing in from the valley, and must not be contaminated. This wind makes me brittle and parched and although the sweat evaporates quickly from my back and forehead it brings no relief; even the juice of my eyes and the mucus in the back of my throat begins to dry up. I veer towards the seafront but the sea air just makes it worse, throwing its grit into my open wounds until I feel like a piece of salted meat hung up to mature. I welcome the pain the way only the guilty can, as if it will absolve me of my sins to be in hot discomfort. It is my brother I want to see me suffer and to watch closely how my eyes sting and my throat burns. He is haunting me. I feel his scorn as clearly as I feel my own blood beat, I sense his anger as close to me as my breath, I know his sadness the way I know hunger. I do not feel his presence beside me like a shadow – I feel inhabited by it, as if he looks with my eyes and feels with my hands. It is a figment, I know – brought on by my raging guilt and hallucinated willingly by my mind. But when he is within my head he whispers things to me from the deep insides of my ears so that they travel outwards and could be heard emerging from my lobes by somebody standing next to me. Over and over he whispers that I have failed him. It is the truth of it that is making me go mad.

I came to the city to kill the President. I looked for a way to put my hands on him – to touch him every day as part of my job, to lull him with my fingertips like a snake charmer hypnotizes with a flute, to pierce his inner circle of security through the deftness of my skill, perform for him an unalarming service, at its essence manual and thus reassuring. And I found that way, and put my hands on him, and every day I held the slim blade of the shaving razor to his throat and could not find the will to slit it (or perhaps will lets me off too easily, it was the courage I could not find). I feared the consequences too much to be able to take my revenge, to avenge your death, brother. I had not yet seen the detail of your disfigurement, the exact nature of the pain he ordered somebody to inflict on your face, the grotesqueness of your death, as I saw it blown up and plastered onto the window of my shop yesterday. But I suspect it would have made little difference: I am a coward, and I wanted to live more than I desired vengeance.

Each time I finished with the President I would return to my shop and my little room and swear to myself I would kill him the next day, and then I would clean fiendishly, and purge and purify myself by curling belts and folding caps and polishing buttons and putting jars upon jars of other people's hair onto shelves according to the shade of their strands, from jet to nut to amber to auburn to pale gold. I was not always like this – before you disappeared I don't remember ever feeling such a strong desire to scrub at my body in the bath until I bled, the way I would after each failed session at the Residence. She thinks I worked for him because I hated you for soaking up our mother's attention like bread in water, that I wanted to groom and pamper the President in thanks for what he did to you. But how could I hate you for being our mother's favourite? You were my god too, and a man cannot be jealous of a god. And then there is her, your first and only lover, whose body I now feel on top of me, whose hair falls into my mouth, whose legs curl around my back to pull me closer. I plead guilty, again, but hear me out: I love her the way you did, she is the only pure thing in my life. I cannot ever replace you and I will forever carry the burden of wondering if she closes her eyes when she feels me lower myself onto her and imagines it is you, but what we have done is the only good thing I have done in my life and I ask your forgiveness but I will not give her up. And now you must leave me alone, because there is nothing else I can do for you, and no way to atone – so leave me here at the City Residence gate and do not come back to me. I beg you.

The guard radios somebody else when I tell him my purpose, receives confirmation, opens the side gate. I walk along the avenue up to the main entrance with my tools in a black carrybag like a doctor making a house visit. The Residence gardens have not changed – the same curt flowerbeds and clipped fruit trees and circumscribed trees – of course, what would one expect? Another guard at the front entrance to the Residence looks through my bag suspiciously, picks out the razor and holds it up to the sun as if to divine its purpose. He radios somebody, is told to let me in and reluctantly holds open the heavy door for me. The foyer is cool and dark and soothing to my eyes. I climb the staircase to the first floor, catching a whiff of my own odour from the effort of my journey and hastily brushing the sweat from my forehead into my hair to disguise it. Another guard stands before the bedroom door, expecting me, holding the door open, and he follows me into the room. I am determined not to look at the bed – their bed. I know it is on my left, at the periphery of my vision. But as I approach the bathroom I cannot resist its pull on my eyeballs and I turn my head to stare at it and wonder which side she sleeps on, and whether he waits until she is asleep to make his advances or demands succour in the fog of morning. When last did the servants change the sheets and pillow slips? Does she refuse him now? Does she have a choice?

The Commander is waiting for me in the bathroom, this time

on the chair I brought especially to the Residence the first time I groomed the President. It puts his head at the level of my chest so that when he leans back onto the headrest his neck will be exposed and will give me the best angle for a close shave. There is an excitement about him today, the impatience of a small boy awaiting a gift. It is early afternoon, but he is barefoot and in his bathrobe, with a faint white stain of dried toothpaste down the front of the lapel. He barely greets me, waves to the guard to wait outside the bathroom, and almost greedily puts on the plastic apron I hand him to keep the soap from dripping onto his chest. He closes his eyes and lies back expectantly with a deep sigh before I have even laid out my implements beside the basin. I look closely at his face and neck: the stubble is blue and some hairs have curled back on themselves and tried to burrow beneath his skin, ingrown and red. Small white scars stand out beneath the stubble, past injuries, self-inflicted – all men know the horror of slitting one's own throat with a razor, no matter how small the wound or how little it bleeds. I notice things about him that I missed the last time: the yellow grease of ear wax hidden within the whorl of his ear, grey bristles venturing out of one nostril, a mole on his chin that has been sliced off so often by shaving it has become aggressively mutant. I wet the brush, massage it in tight circles against the soap until it foams thickly, then use the same circular motion with the brush against his skin, the cream lathering and growing in volume until his cheeks and chin and neck are covered by it.

I hear the bedroom door open and a woman's sandals clicking across the floor – her sandals, the sound of her dress swishing against her knees. Before I can turn to the doorway she is inside the bathroom, and the guard murmurs a greeting to her then turns away, and she looks at me with her eyes bright and sad as a small bird's.

The Commander does not open his, but lifts an arm lazily as if to acknowledge her, and says, 'We're busy, darling. Did you really have to bother us?'

She looks down at her feet, then walks quickly to the cupboard beneath the basin and kneels beside it. 'I forgot something,' she says, and rummages amongst the bottles and vials and boxes. 'I'll be quick.'

I watch her hands as they search, so delicate, so assured. And then I see them: six new wounds on the inside of her left arm, raw and fresh, identical to the scars on her right, a sick symmetry of pain. The circles of flesh are raised and blistered. In places the wet scab has split and released clear liquid. She has not dressed them – they are unbandaged, untended, infected. She looks at me suddenly, closes the cupboard, and leaves the room empty-handed. I hear her opening a drawer in the bedroom. The Commander still has not opened his eyes.

It is then that I lift the blade from beside the basin and split open his neck like a soft fruit until I reach his oesophagus. The blood seeps more slowly than I expected into the white foam and his head slumps forward until his nose rests against his sternum; his lips are pressed to his own collarbone. The foam is now frothy and pink.

I pack up my utensils carefully, put each one in its proper place in the bag, rinse the knife, turn on the shower, and close the bathroom door quietly behind me.

'Showering,' I say to the guard, and he nods and looks bored and wanders out onto the balcony. I walk slowly towards her, to where she sits at the edge of the bed, lift her left arm, turn it, kiss each wet wound softly, then take her hand and lead her gently out of the room. She looks back once, towards the bathroom, but grips my hand. I feel nothing but conviction. They are all the same, these men, and it is best to nip them in the bud.

2 *His portraitist*

I was not allowed into the room while my wife was in labour with our child. The guards let me wait outside the door, but the sounds of her agony fought their way beneath it and made me want to tear my ears from my head and rip my own stomach open if it could only ease her pain. The President's wife was let in to be her midwife, with a napkin held to her chin that my wife had split open in the throes of her pain. She gave me a dark look as she passed me – the first time she has looked at me with anything but lust in her eyes. The thought that I had ever let her touch me, that our bare skins had ever slid across each other, made me sick. The labour took a day and half the night. The guards told me to sleep, but how could I while she moaned like a sick animal so close to me, thinking as each scream faded that I had done this to her? I glimpsed her once, when the doctor called for more hot water and the President's wife opened the door to receive it from the guard. She was lying curled up like a baby on the bed, mimicking the position our own child was in, with her knees drawn up to her stomach and her eyes closed and her mouth set in such grim determination I barely recognized her. The doctor was trying to swing her legs down and open and place her feet against the bottom of the bedstead, but she only clenched them more tightly together. It was only then that I began to worry about the child. Until then I had thought only of my wife, and longed for her pain to be over, whatever the consequences, but I saw the panic in the doctor's face and fear for my child became a dull thudding in my gut.

Night fell slowly. I felt the dusk's beauty as an insult. I could see the rose bushes glowing and the statues' shadows as they thinned and I saw my wife lying on the grass on her back with her legs in the air, stretching, and my love for her made me promise all kinds of things to myself, things I would never do again if she could only survive this, things I would do for her every day if she could endure. When the light had faded and the statues loomed like threats in the blackness I am ashamed to say that I would even have promised my firstborn to anybody who asked for it, if it would have guaranteed my wife's survival. There is a crippling desperation to being a man when a wife gives birth. I did not realize how low I could be forced to stoop – that I could promise such an unnatural thing, to hand away my own flesh in a dank deal with the spirits of my mind. And then it wailed, a rattle-blood cry, a howl to the moon. I would never have believed a child that had just been through such trauma could have the lungs to yell its way into life like that.

The President's wife came to the door and spoke through it: 'It's a boy. She is fine, just exhausted. Go to bed now, you cannot see them until the morning.'

I hugged the guard, and he pulled away from me awkwardly and shifted his feet. I ran into the rose garden and rolled on the grass with delight and climbed on top of one of the statues and leapt from it into the darkness, and cried and wept and laughed until the guard pulled me up and told me to go back to my room. My back was wet with dew and my hand began to bleed from the rosebush thorns and my ankle felt strange from the way I landed and even my kidneys began to pulse their old warning, but I felt none of it as pain until I woke this morning in my bed and noticed the blood smears on my pillow and felt the thud, thud of my thickened ankle and the tension in my kidneys. And then I remembered I had a child, a tiny new baby boy, and it was rapturous to lie there with that precious, warm thought in my head and let my mind suck on it like a sweet under my tongue.

I washed ritually before leaving the room this morning, as a private tribute to my wife. I wanted to cleanse myself of all my past sins and soaked in the bathwater for a long time to soften my pores so that they would release all their grime. The water was grey when I let it out. I combed my hair, trimmed my fingernails, shaved, and put on my last clean shirt. As I walked along the corridor overlooking the rose garden, I looked down and saw the bush I had damaged in my leap from the statue, and the grass I had flattened with my back. I walked slowly down the stairs, admiring the pattern of the iron banister the sun threw on the wall, and along the passageway to her door. Several guards were posted outside and stiffened when they saw me coming. One of them told me I could not see her in her bedroom, that I was to wait in the room where I painted the Commander's portrait and that she and the child would be brought to me there.

I have been waiting for over an hour in this room. The couch where I sat beside the President has been pushed against the wall, and several chairs have been brought in and placed in a semicircle around it, as if expecting an audience. I cannot understand why I have been forced to wait here to see her and the child. I hate thinking of her having to climb the stairs with the ache that she must have between her legs – surely she is weak and wounded and should be allowed to rest. The room is stuffy; the windows are closed despite the rising heat outside. I pull back the curtains and unclasp the latch and slide open the window, but there is no wind today to bring cool relief. The air hangs still and obstinate just outside the frame, refusing to move, and the valley shimmers colourlessly in the heat.

I hear voices and go to the door impatiently. The President is being led by three guards down the corridor towards me, his hands bound in front of him, his jowls hanging as low as a wolf's, his head droopy. He does not look at me as he shuffles into the room, nor when he is made to sit on the couch against the wall. The guards pay me no attention and ignore my questions. I start to feel dizzy, like a dog chasing its own tail, and go to the window again to breathe more deeply and try to slow my heartbeat. Fear grips my entrails again – they are already bruised from last night's desperation, but the new fear is relentless; something is going horribly wrong, there is an arena being set up here before my eyes and I know I am going to be asked to witness something horrific and I feel sure it will involve the child. One of the guards stands next to the couch, the other slumps into one of the chairs facing him, the third leaves the room. More voices. The sweat is collecting in the small of my back now, my pulse is racing, the veins on my hands and arms are engorged.

The President's wife is led into the room, and as she sees her husband she pushes the guard away and stumbles to him and kisses his face and skull and puts her face in his lap and cries. He does nothing – he barely looks at her – and the guard pulls her off and makes her sit in one of the chairs facing the President. She blows kisses at him through her tears and whispers endearments to him, but he does not even raise his eyes.

The third guard closes the door and clears his throat. 'The Commander wanted to be here today,' he says, glancing at the President. 'But it seems he has been tied up in the city.'

He pauses, looks slightly uncomfortable. I watch the sweat marks forming beneath his armpits, spreading against his shirt. Then he opens the door. My wife is standing outside, holding our baby. The child is naked, and she is barely clothed, in a nightdress that is transparent in the morning sun, and her nipples have leaked onto the front of the dress. I start to run towards her, but the guard steps in my way and holds me back, and as she takes an unsteady step into the room, the baby begins to squeal its hunger.

I stop struggling and watch her walk slowly towards the President. Her face seems fleshless; her eyes do not seek me out. She reaches him and kneels before him, her knee bones cracking against the hard floor, and lays the baby in his lap. I see its face for the first time: its forehead is vast, its eyes are too close together.

'Your son,' she says to him, then she spits in his slack face.

3 *His chef*

I told him anyway, even after what she let me do to her in their bathroom; I told her husband what she and the barber had been up to, lurking in the bushes, seamy looks, sly desires; that she would come home smelling of him and corrupt their sheets with his stench. He had no idea – how he could have missed it is beyond me, but perhaps my sense of smell is more acute after so many years of infidelity. I can always smell another man on a woman, beneath the soaps and lotions and perfumes they use to mask it. That barber was too quick for him, it seems – but not quick enough, however. The guards outside rounded the two of them up like a pair of startled cattle, hustled them into the back of a van and drove them to the old revolutionary graveyard in the mountains. I gave particular instructions for them to be killed in just the fashion his brother was. I like the symmetry of it.

Why they left through the front door and walked straight into the trap confounds me – if the barber knew of the Commander's plan to capture him, and killed him because of it, why did they not escape through the back? There were no guards there, and she would have known the way out. The Commander's guard only realized what the barber had done hours later, when the Commander's shower had seemed to go on for ever, when the steam was so thick in the bedroom he could barely see his own hand before his face, and he risked all censure and opened the bathroom door cautiously, despite receiving no permission to enter. My men acted quickly to stem any protests, but there were not many, just confusion. It was worth the trouble it took to gain their loyalty these past months. They knew the Commander favoured me, that I had been his eyes when he could not see; they liked that I had no previous political experience (they are ignorant of the tyranny of an executive chef in his kitchens), that I would bring attention to detail (the exact placement of garnish on a plate) and respect for due process (mincing, grating, blanching) to the position. It has been a smooth transition.

I've moved into the master bedroom already, and the bathroom has been mopped and bleached, and the balcony door has been left open to air out the room, but I asked that the sheets not be changed. I wanted to sleep for just one night on her side of the bed, with my nose against her pillow. I am sorry to lose her, but she would not have taken kindly to my betrayal, and, in time, there will be others – other women, other betrayals.

My daughter was still here when it happened. She had come to find me at the Residence, pretending to be searching for work. I sent her back to the home when the Commander's body was discovered, fearing violence, but it turned out to be an unnecessary precaution and I sent word for her to pack her bags and leave her mother in the home (the bill will be paid) and arrange her things in the bedroom furthest down the hall from mine, with the view of the seafront. I have promised her that her little lover can move in here too, if we can find him – the President's son. She was horrified that I knew about it, but I didn't read her diary for nothing. It will take some explaining to my men, but he can always pretend ignorance, shock, horror, and so forth, about what his father did – the children can usually get away with it, and my men will accept it and he can move in and they can continue their strange affair under my roof. It amuses me that she becomes more like me each day.

She moved into the Residence today. When I saw her I could sense she was trying to restrain herself, to withhold some emotion, but she failed and ran towards me with tears streaming down her face, and jumped into my arms with her hands around my neck and would not let go. She tries so hard to hate me, to deny to herself that we are more similar than she would like, but there is too much of me in her to resist it. She sobbed into my shoulder for a long time.

I felt such tenderness for her suddenly and I remembered the weight of her head against my neck when she was a tiny baby. It was a shock to me to have a baby daughter: I was surprised at how sorry I felt for all the terrible things I had done to women in my life – they were baby daughters too, once, and their fathers had held their soft heads against their necks and wished feverishly to protect them from all harm, if only for a moment – and I had paid their wishes no attention and used them in ways to make a father's blood run cold.

The compunction didn't last long. In this kind of place, it rarely does.

Huge thanks to my editor, Sarah Castleton, and to Toby Mundy, Karen Duffy and Daniel Scott at Atlantic Books. I'm also deeply grateful to Sarah Chalfant, Charles Buchan and Edward Orloff.